Batter Royale

by Leisl Adams

AMULET BOOKS • NEW YORK

PUBLISHER'S NOTE: This is a work of fiction. Names, characters, places, and incidents are either the product of the author's imagination or used fictitiously, and any resemblance to actual persons, living or dead, business establishments, events, or locales is entirely coincidental.

Library of Congress Cataloging Number for the hardcover edition: 2021941588

Hardcover ISBN 978-1-4197-5075-5
Paperback ISBN 978-1-4197-5076-2

Colors by Andrew Dalhouse
Book design by Andrea Miller

Published in 2022 by Amulet Books, an imprint of ABRAMS.

Printed and bound in China
10 9 8 7 6 5 4 3 2 1

Amulet Books are available at special discounts when purchased in quantity for premiums and promotions as well as fundraising or educational use. Special editions can also be created to specification. For details, contact specialsales@abramsbooks.com or the address below.

Amulet Books® is a registered trademark of Harry N. Abrams, Inc.

ABRAMS The Art of Books
195 Broadway, New York, NY 10007
abramsbooks.com

To my dad, who said,
if anyone could do it, you can

6:00
GOOD MORNING!
DID YOU EVEN SIGN THOSE PAPERS YET—
I'LL GET TO IT!

WERE YOU GUYS ARGUING AGAIN?

NO! NO! NOT AT ALL!
WE WERE JUST TALKING, HON!

I'LL BE AT THE OFFICE LATE TONIGHT.
BYE, DAD!
THERE'S NOT MUCH THERE, BUT I'LL GET A FEW GROCERIES ON THE WAY HOME.
OH, IT'S NO PROBLEM. I'LL WHIP SOMETHING UP.
YOU ALWAYS DO! DON'T BE LATE FOR SCHOOL. AND DON'T FORGET YOUR COLLEGE APPLICATIONS!

APPLE
BUTTER
SPLASH OF ORANGE JUICE
COOK
CRUMBLE
TOAST IN OVEN

8:30
FINALLY!

9:00
ACK! GONNA BE LATE!

- 1 apple, peeled, cored, and chopped

- 1 tablespoon butter

- 1 teaspoon orange or lemon juice
- 1 teaspoon brown sugar
- ¼ teaspoon cinnamon
- water (optional): add 1 teaspoon at a time to make a sauce

Directions

1. Preheat oven to 350°F. Prepare a ramekin or oven-safe bowl with cooking spray or butter.
2. Place all ingredients in a pan on medium heat. Cook for 5 minutes or until apples are soft.

- ¼ cup flour
- ¼ cup quick oats
- 2 tablespoons softened butter
- ½ teaspoon cinnamon
- ¼ cup brown sugar

1. Place all ingredients in a medium bowl. Using a fork, mash all ingredients together until crumbly.
2. Transfer cooked apples to buttered and floured bowl or ramekin.

3. Add crumble mixture to top. Bake for 20 minutes.

TIPS

- Get fancy by adding ice cream, whipped cream, or caramel!
- You can experiment with different apples for different flavors and textures! I like McIntosh best!

SIGH
LATE AGAIN, ROSE?
SORRY, MA'AM!

APPLY TO ANY COLLEGES YET?
JUST ONE ACTUALLY. I DON'T KNOW IF I CAN AFFORD IT THOUGH.
HAHA, REALLY? I'VE APPLIED TO LIKE, FIVE!

ATLANTIC LOBSTER
$8
QUAYGA
DINER + TAKE OUT

AFTERNOON, ROSE! YOU'VE BEEN LATE A LOT RECENTLY. EVERYTHING OKAY?
EVERYTHING'S FINE; IT'S ONLY TEN MINUTES!
THE BOSS ISN'T GONNA LIKE IT!
IT'S FINE, WE GO WAY BACK!

HEY, FRED!

OH, HEY, UH . . .
HOW YA DOIN'?
GOOD. YOU?

I'M OKAY. MUM'S JUST CALLED A MEETING FOR THE KITCHEN STAFF. I THINK SHE'S LETTING A FEW PEOPLE GO . . . SHE CAN'T AFFORD TO KEEP THEM.

AT THIS RATE I'LL BE STUCK HERE FOREVER.
OOOH, DO YOU THINK SHE COULD USE SOME HELP WITH FOOD PREP?
YOU COULD GIVE IT A SHOT!

NICE OF YOU TO JOIN US, ROSE! TEN MINUTES LATE THIS TIME?
HOW DID SHE KNOW!
YEAH . . . SORRY ABOUT THAT, BONNIE! I MEAN, MA'AM!
I MEAN, CHEF!
SO UM, I WAS WONDERING, SINCE YOU'RE SHORT ON STAFF TODAY, IF YOU KNOW, MAYBE . . . I COULD HELP IN THE KITCHEN . . . A BIT?

I CAN'T HAVE KITCHEN STAFF ARRIVING LATE, SO THANKS, BUT NOT TODAY.
OH, OKAY, NO WORRIES!

ATLANTIC LOBSTER $8
QUAYGA
DINER + TAKE OUT

HEY, ROSE! I COULD USE SOME HELP CLEANING UP THE KITCHEN WHEN YOU'RE DONE.
REALLY?!
YOU LOOK LIKE YOU'VE NEVER SEEN THE KITCHEN BEFORE.
WELL, I DON'T GET TO HANG OUT IN HERE MUCH!
I FEEL LIKE I WAS BORN IN HERE. IT'S REALLY NOT THAT EXCITING.

I FEEL LIKE MAKING SOMETHING. DON'T YOU?
W-WHAT?
WAIT. NO. WE NEED TO CLEAN UP AND HEAD HOME, THOSE WERE MY INSTRUCTIONS.
COME ON! FASTEST DESSERT WINS. IT'LL TAKE LIKE, TWENTY MINUTES TOPS!
ARE YOU SERIOUS? WE'RE ALMOST DONE CLEANING!
WE'LL BARELY MAKE A MESS!
THIS IS A BAD IDEA.
HAVE A LITTLE FUN FOR ONCE! BESIDES, YOUR MOM WON'T BE BACK FOR WHAT, ANOTHER HALF HOUR?
FINE. FIFTEEN MINUTES. AND WE HAVE TO HAVE THE PLACE CLEAN BEFORE SHE'S BACK.
YESSSS!

I COULD WHIP UP A CHOCOLATE MOUSSE.
NAH, TOO BORING . . .
OR MAYBE, TRUFFLES?
ROSE!
TWELVE MORE MINUTES!
RIGHT! RIGHT!

I'M SO GONNA WIN THIS.
IN YOUR DREAMS!
YOU PROBABLY SHOULD HAVE DONE THOSE A BIT SOONER.
HOW DO YOU EVEN KNOW WHAT I'M MAKING? WERE YOU WATCHING ME?
UH, NO. OF COURSE NOT. JUST KIDDING AROUND.

GIGGLE

SO, WHAT ARE YOU DOING AFTER SCHOOL IS OVER?

WELL, I'VE BEEN THINKING ABOUT TRAVELING FOR A BIT.
OH . . .
I'D COME VISIT YOU THOUGH, I MEAN, WHEREVER YOU END UP GOING!
THAT WOULD BE NICE.
ALTHOUGH, WE'VE BEEN FRIENDS SINCE WE WERE KIDS. WHAT'S A FEW MONTHS, RIGHT?
RIGHT!

TA-DA!!!
HEY, I WAS GONNA MAKE THAT!
FRED!!

ROSE. YOU CAN GO HOME NOW.
IT'S MY FAULT, CHEF—
WE'LL TALK LATER, ROSE.
YOU, YOUNG MAN, ARE GOING TO HELP ME CLEAN THIS UP.
YES, MUM, ER, CHEF.

Chocolate Truffles

Makes 8 to 10 truffles

Directions

1. Mix cream cheese, chocolate baking crumbs, and powdered sugar together in a bowl.
2. Roll approximately 1 teaspoon of the mixture at a time into individual balls.
3. Cover in cocoa powder or melted chocolate and sea salt, then refrigerate until ready to serve.

FRED'S CHOCOLATE Mousse

SERVES 2

½ cup chocolate chips

½ heavy whipping cream

Directions

1. Place ingredients in a microwave-safe bowl.
2. Microwave in 20-seconds increments until chocolate chips start to melt.
3. Whisk until combined, then refrigerate mix until cool.
4. Once cooled, use a hand or stand mixer to whip until stiff peaks form.

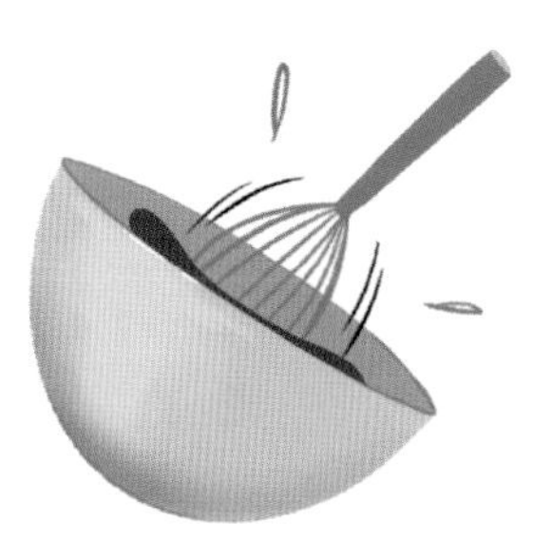

5. Spoon into individual bowls or glasses.

MOM! DAD! YOU WON'T BELIEVE THIS!

I GOT IN! I GOT INTO FIELDBERRY!
THAT'S WONDERFUL, HONEY!
IS DAD WORKING IN HIS OFFICE?
PROBABLY.
FIELDBERRY CULINARY SCHOOL:
THIS IS LIKE, THE BEST COOKING SCHOOL! IT'S GONNA BE SO AWESOME!
FIELDBERRY
THAT TUITION THOUGH!

WE CAN FIGURE IT OUT.
ARE YOU KIDDING? WE DON'T HAVE THAT KIND OF MONEY!
I'M GONNA GO . . . FINISH UP SOME HOMEWORK.
SHE REALLY WANTS THIS; LET'S NOT DISMISS IT RIGHT AWAY.
BUT WHEN WE FACTOR IN THE DORM, LIVING EXPENSES . . .
YOU ALWAYS DO THIS! SOMETHING GOOD HAPPENS AND YOU GO STRAIGHT INTO TALKING ABOUT MONEY.
WE HAVE TO BE REALISTIC. I DON'T WANT TO GET HER HOPES UP.

THE NEXT DAY. . .
HEY! HOW WAS GEOGRAPHY?
OH, YOU KNOW, CURRENT EVENTS, FOOD DISTRIBUTION, AND STUFF. IT'S PRETTY INTERESTING! I'D LOVE TO VISIT SOME OF THOSE PLACES.
NERD!
ARE YOU OKAY?

I KNEW YOU WERE UPSET! MY MOM CAN BE TOO HARSH SOMETIMES—
IT'S NOT THAT!
WHAT? WHAT IS IT?
MY PARENTS HAD A FIGHT LAST NIGHT. EVERYTHING AT HOME IS SO WEIRD.
OH CRAP, THAT SUCKS, ROSE! IS THERE ANYTHING I CAN DO TO HELP?

WELL, I WAS KINDA WONDERING ABOUT MY JOB, AND WHETHER OR NOT I STILL HAVE ONE. IT'S KIND OF MY ONLY ESCAPE RIGHT NOW, PLUS I NEED THE MONEY.
I'M SURE ONCE YOU APOLOGIZE AND PROMISE TO BE MORE RESPONSIBLE, YOU'LL BE FINE!
IS THAT WHAT YOU DID?
NAH, I'M HER SON, I HAD TO BEG FOR MY LIFE.
ACTUALLY, I'M ON POTATO-PEELING DUTY FOR A WEEK.
HA! HA! HA!
THIS MIGHT MAKE YOU FEEL BETTER. I MANAGED TO SWIPE OUR DESSERTS!
YOU DID? NICE WORK!
THANKS!

MENU
UH, CHEF BONNIE?
I . . . I JUST WANTED TO APOLOGIZE FOR LAST NIGHT . . .
DO YOU?
YES?

I KNOW WE SHOULD'VE BEEN HELPING TO CLEAN UP, AND IT WAS MY FAULT BECAUSE I WANTED TO TRY MY HAND AT MAKING SOMETHING IN THE KITCHEN AND WE SORTA LOST TRACK OF TIME AND I'M REALLY, REALLY SORRY AND I PROMISE TO BE MORE PROFESSIONAL IN THE FUTURE—
ROSE!
I **UNDERSTAND!**
I **KNOW** YOU WANT TO BE IN THE KITCHEN!
YOU AND FRED HAVE BEEN FRIENDS SINCE YOU WERE KIDS, BUT HE'S BEEN IN THIS KITCHEN HIS WHOLE LIFE, AND YOU'VE ONLY JUST STARTED.

I BELIEVE YOU CAN DO IT, BUT I NEED YOU TO BE MORE RESPONSIBLE! NO MORE ARRIVING LATE, AND NO MORE COOKING AFTER HOURS WITHOUT PERMISSION.

YOU'RE MY BEST SERVER. FOR NOW, I NEED YOU TO STAY OUT FRONT. LEARN THE ROPES! THERE'S MORE TO RUNNING A KITCHEN THAN JUST COOKING.

OKAY, CHEF!

DID YOU HEAR SOMETHING ABOUT A FOOD CRITIC COMING TODAY?
YUP, DARLA MCQUEEN. SHE'S DOING A REVIEW FOR HER MAGAZINE. BONNIE SEEMS PRETTY NERVOUS.
YEAH, IT'S PRETTY MUCH MAKE OR BREAK FOR THIS PLACE.
WE'LL SEE.
WHAT? IS THAT TRUE?
MY MUM MAY HAVE MENTIONED SOMETHING ABOUT IT. REVIEWS HAPPEN ALL THE TIME, WHAT'S THE BIG DEAL?
ARE YOU KIDDING? DARLA IS LIKE A **MAJOR** LEAGUE RESTAURANT CRITIC AND BAKER! A GOOD REVIEW FROM HER WOULD MEAN MORE CUSTOMERS. DUDE, YOU **NEED** TO READ MORE INDUSTRY MAGAZINES.
WHAT I **NEED** TO DO IS FINISH THIS ENGLISH ESSAY.

UM, ROSE? YOU'RE MAKING THAT WEIRD FACE YOU ALWAYS MAKE WHEN YOU COME UP WITH A BAD IDEA.

WHAT IF WE **ADDED** A *NEW* DESSERT FOR HER TO SAMPLE? I KNOW WHAT SHE'LL **LOVE!**
WHAT? **NO!**

ARE YOU KIDDING? THIS ISN'T A GAME; THE RESTAURANT IS ALREADY IN ENOUGH TROUBLE AS IT IS!

OKAY! OKAY! I GET IT.

CRASH!

JEN! YOU OKAY?
TIPS

YEAH, JUST NOT MY DAY TODAY.
YOU'VE GOT A CUT.
MARIA, COULD YOU TAKE OVER FOR A SECOND?
EXIT

LET'S GET YOU TO THE WASH STATION.
THANKS, ROSE, YOU WERE A BIG HELP.
NO PROBLEM!

SOOO . . . HAVE YOU GIVEN ANY MORE THOUGHT TO MY IDEA?
HMM?
YOU KNOW, THE DESSERT! TO WIN OVER THAT CRITIC?
NO! WHY ARE YOU ASKING FOR MORE TROUBLE AFTER WHAT HAPPENED LAST TIME?
FRED?
MEETING'S STARTING!
FORGET ABOUT IT, ROSE!

WHAT THE HECK ARE YOU DOING?
JUST GETTING SOME INGREDIENTS!
I ONLY NEED A FEW MINUTES. I KNOW THE PERFECT DESSERT FOR DARLA—A STRAWBERRY SHORTCAKE!
I JUST NEED YOU TO MAKE A DIVERSION!
I CAN'T HELP YOU! I'LL BE PEELING POTATOES FOR THE REST OF MY LIFE!

D-DON'T GO IN THERE!
WHY?
UMM . . .
I THINK I SAW A MOUSE. DON'T TELL CHEF! DO WE HAVE ANY TRAPS?
I'LL GO CHECK THE BACK.
SHE'S GONE!
WHO'S GONE?

UHH... THE UH...
MOUSE! THERE WAS A MOUSE, BUT I THINK SHE'S GONE, HEH.
GREAT! THAT'S ALL WE NEED. I'LL CALL THE EXTERMINATOR.
LATER . . .
HURRY, HURRY . . .

YOU LOOKING FOR SOMETHING?
UH, A CUSTOMER WAS JUST ASKING ABOUT HOT SAUCE. GOT ANY?

THANKS.

QUAYGA
WHAT'S GOING ON?
SHE'S ALL YOURS!
QUAYGA DINER
WHAT? ME? WHY?

HI, AND WELCOME TO THE QUAYGA DINER! CAN I GET YOU A DRINK TO START?

QUAYGA
DINER
ACTUALLY, CAN I SEE THE DESSERT MENU DEAR?

SURE! SURE, OF COURSE.
I HEAR THIS PLACE HAS SOME ACE DESSERTS.
OH YEAH! THE BEST IN TOWN!
HMM . . .
QUAYGA DINER
I'VE DECIDED TO GIVE THEM ALL A GO.
QUAYGA DINER
SURE . . . I WILL GET THAT FOR YOU . . . ALL OF THEM . . . COMING RIGHT UP.

QUAYGA DINER
HOPEFULLY THIS'LL GET HER ATTENTION.
PROBLEM?

NOPE! EVERYTHING'S FINE!
HEY, COULD YOU SERVE THIS TO THE CRITIC, WHILE I GO TO THE BATHROOM FOR A SEC?
SURE!

WILL THERE BE ANYTHING ELSE?
JUST THE BILL PLEASE . . . OH, AND MAY I SPEAK TO THE CHEF?
SURE, NO PROBLEM.

HI, I'M BONNIE FERGUSON! OWNER AND HEAD CHEF.
I'M DARLA MCQUEEN, FOOD CRITIC FOR *SWEET NOTHINGS* MAGAZINE. I JUST WANTED TO SAY THAT YOUR DESSERTS REALLY ARE WONDERFUL!
THANKS—
ESPECIALLY THAT LAST ONE THAT WASN'T ON THE MENU. WHAT A SURPRISE!
THE LAST ONE . . . ?
DID YOU MAKE THAT ONE YOURSELF?
WELL, JIM AND MY SON FRED WERE ON DESSERTS . . .
UM, CHEF, NEITHER OF US MADE THAT ONE.
THEN WHO DID?

YES! THAT'S ROSE, ONE OF MY BEST SERVERS . . .
. . . THOUGH YOU'VE BEEN A BIT OFF YOUR GAME LATELY.
SHE LOVES EXPERIMENTING IN THE KITCHEN!
HEH. HI!
A SERVER WHO ALSO DOES DESSERTS. THIS IS GREAT STUFF!
HAVE A SEAT!

SO ROSE, TELL ME ABOUT YOURSELF.
WELL, UM, I'M A HIGH SCHOOL SENIOR.
I WANT TO GO TO COOKING SCHOOL. I'D REALLY LOVE TO BE A PASTRY CHEF AND RUN MY OWN RESTAURANT SOMEDAY.
HMM, WONDERFUL, WHAT ABOUT YOUR PERSONAL LIFE?
PERSONAL LIFE?

YES, WHAT ABOUT LIFE AT HOME? YOUR FAMILY? A BOYFRIEND?
UM . . . UH . . . NO BOYFRIEND. THERE'S MY MOM AND DAD . . . THEY'RE NOT DOING SO WELL RIGHT NOW.

I'M SORRY TO HEAR THAT.
HOW DO YOU FEEL ABOUT FOOD COMPETITIONS?

I'VE SEEN A FEW ON TV . . .

I'M PRODUCING A SHOW CALLED *BATTER ROYALE* AND LOOKING FOR CONTESTANTS. YOU MAY BE THE RIGHT FIT.
ME? ON A TV SHOW?
IT WOULD ONLY BE ONE WEEK. WE PROVIDE ROOM AND BOARD.
I DUNNO . . .
JUDGING BY YOUR DESSERT, I REALLY DO THINK YOU HAVE WHAT IT TAKES.
THE GRAND PRIZE IS HALF A MILLION DOLLARS AND A BOOK DEAL.

THE ONLY THING IS YOU NEED A TEAMMATE.
WELL, UM . . .
BONNIE?
I'M FLATTERED, BUT A FOOD COMPETITION IS THE LAST THING I HAVE TIME FOR.
WELL, IF YOU MANAGE TO FIND A PARTNER, THE SHOW IS RECORDED IN LONDON IN TWO MONTHS. YOU THINK ABOUT IT AND LET ME KNOW IF YOU'RE INTERESTED.
OPEN

Vanilla Strawberry Shortcake

SERVES 8

⅔ cup cold butter, cubed

2 cups flour

1 teaspoon baking powder

FOR THE Cake

2 tablespoons sugar

⅔ cup buttermilk

1 egg

Milk or egg whites, for brushing

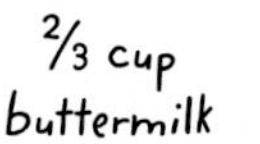

Directions

1. Preheat oven to 425ºF. Place the cubed butter and flour into a bowl and cut together with a fork until mixture becomes crumbly.

2. Add the baking powder and sugar. Combine the buttermilk and egg in a separate container, then make a well in the center of the dry ingredients. Pour the wet ingredients into the well, then combine to form a dough.

3. Tip dough onto a floured surface and roll it out until it is approximately 1 inch thick.

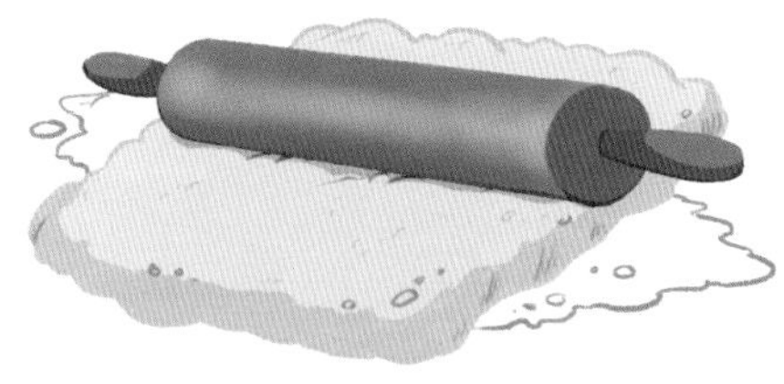

4. Use a glass or round cutter to cut out round shapes. Transfer to a baking sheet and brush the tops with milk or egg whites.

5. Bake for 15 minutes or until golden.

FOR THE Strawberries

2 cups strawberries

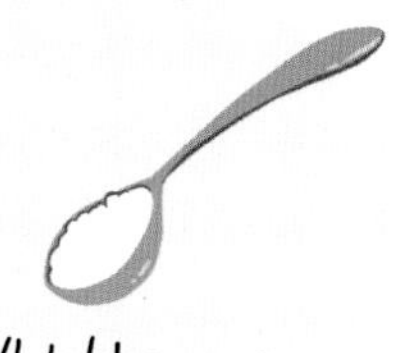

4 tablespoons sugar

Directions

1. Remove tops from strawberries and slice (leave 4 or 5 whole). Place into a small bowl, coat with the sugar, and set aside.

FOR THE Topping

1 cup heavy whipping cream

½ teaspoon vanilla

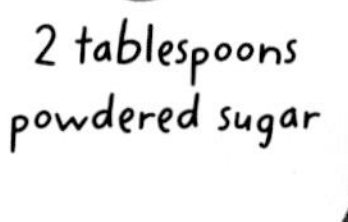

2 tablespoons powdered sugar

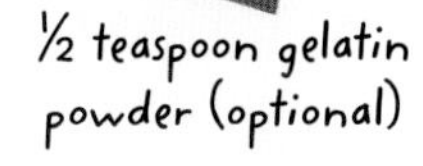

½ teaspoon gelatin powder (optional)

Directions

1. If using gelatin, dissolve the gelatin powder in 1 tablespoon of hot water and set aside.
2. Using a hand blender or mixer with a whisk attachment, beat the heavy whipping cream on low, then slowly turn it up to medium speed. (Add the gelatin mixture as it thickens.)
3. Once the cream starts to hold its shape, add the vanilla and powdered sugar. Turn the speed to high and continue to whip until stiff peaks form.

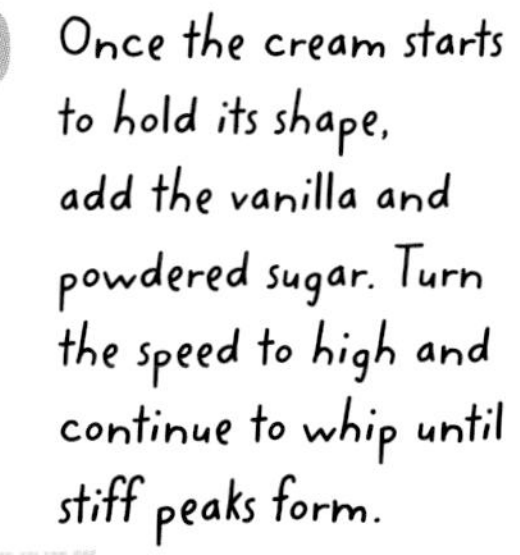

ASSEMBLY

Assemble the cakes by cutting a scone in half and layering strawberries, then whipped cream inside. Place the other half of the scone on top and repeat the layers of strawberries and whipped cream. Place whole strawberries on top.

UNICORN café
COMING SOON
QUAYGA
UNICORN café
DINER ENTRANCE

ONE WEEK LATER . . .
UNICORN café
DINER ENTRANCE
THE BAD NEWS IS, WITH THE NEW CAFÉ ACROSS THE STREET, COMPETITION HAS GOTTEN TOUGH.

BUT I HAVE FULL CONFIDENCE THAT WE CAN BOUNCE BACK FROM THIS! YOU GUYS ARE LIKE FAMILY, AND I APPRECIATE EVERY ONE OF YOU.
IF WE ALL WORK HARD, I THINK WE CAN GET THROUGH THIS. THANK YOU!
MAYBE THERE'S SOMETHING WE CAN DO TO HELP BUSINESS.
LIKE WHAT?
I DUNNO, KARAOKE, TRIVIA NIGHTS, A CONTEST OR SOMETHING?
MAYBE IF I GO ON THAT COOKING SHOW THE PUBLICITY WOULD HELP THE RESTAURANT . . .

MAYBE . . . YOU COULD TEAM UP WITH ME?
C'MON, ROSE.
I'M SERIOUS. I'D ASK ONE OF THE OTHER GUYS, BUT I DON'T THINK THEY LIKE ME VERY MUCH.
YOU HEARD MY MOM EARLIER—SHE'S DEPENDING ON US TO KEEP THIS PLACE GOING. BESIDES, A WORLD-CLASS CONTEST LIKE THAT SEEMS A BIT . . . OUT OF OUR LEAGUE.
NOTHING'S OUT OF YOUR LEAGUE, FRED. YOU JUST HAVE TO, YA KNOW, REACH FOR IT!

I'M SO PROUD OF YOU, HON, I REALLY AM! BUT WE JUST MAY NOT BE ABLE TO AFFORD THIS TUITION.
FIELDBERRY
FIELDBERRY IS ONE OF THE BEST SCHOOLS OUT THERE. I REALLY WANT TO GO!
I KNOW YOU DO, HON. LET'S SEE WHAT SCHOLARSHIPS AND LOANS WE CAN APPLY FOR FIRST.
I MIGHT HAVE A DIFFERENT SOLUTION . . .

I'VE BEEN OFFERED A SPOT ON A COMPETITIVE BAKING SHOW. IT'S FILMING IN LONDON, AND IT'S CALLED *BATTER ROYALE!*
WHAT?
FIRST PLACE IS HALF A MILLION BUCKS AND A BOOK DEAL! AND IT'LL BE ON THE FOOD NETWORK—
WAIT, WAIT, JUST SLOW DOWN A SEC!

WE . . . NEED TO TELL YOU SOMETHING FIRST.

YOU KNOW HOW THINGS HAVE BEEN DIFFICULT BETWEEN YOUR FATHER AND I . . .
YEAH . . .
. . . AND WE TRIED TO KEEP IT TOGETHER, FOR YOU, AND FOR US AS A FAMILY, BUT, WELL—
WE'VE DECIDED TO SEPARATE FOR A WHILE.
WE THINK IT'LL BE BETTER THIS WAY, AT LEAST FOR NOW.

WHY IS THIS HAPPENING NOW? DID I DO SOMETHING?
AWW ROSEMARY, DON'T BLAME YOURSELF. YOU'VE BEEN SO BUSY WITH SCHOOL AND WORK, BUT WE'VE BEEN TALKING ABOUT IT FOR A WHILE.
WE'LL GET THROUGH THIS TOGETHER, OKAY?
IT STILL HURTS LIKE HELL.
I KNOW, AND MONEY WILL BE TIGHT FOR A WHILE, BUT WE'RE GONNA TRY TO MAKE THIS AS EASY AS POSSIBLE.
WE'LL STILL DO HOLIDAYS AND BIRTHDAYS TOGETHER, OKAY?
OKAY.

OH! HEY, ROSE! EVERYTHING OKAY?
UGH. MY PARENTS TOLD ME LAST NIGHT THAT THEY'RE SEPARATING. DAD WILL PROBABLY HAVE LEFT BY THE TIME I GET HOME.

I'M REALLY SORRY ROSE . . .

I'LL BE OKAY . . .

HAVE YOU GIVEN ANY MORE THOUGHT TO THE CONTEST?

ERM . . . I HAVEN'T REALLY THOUGHT ABOUT IT.

NOW DOESN'T SEEM LIKE THE RIGHT TIME TO BE HONEST.

I'D BETTER HEAD TO CLASS BEFORE I'M LATE.
YEAH, SEE YA.

WOW, ROSE, WHAT'S ALL THIS FOR?
I KNOW YOU AND DAD ARE GOING THROUGH A LOT, BUT I'M HOPING YOU'LL STILL GIVE SOME THOUGHT TO THE CONTEST.
OH, ROSE, IT'S ONE THING TO TRAVEL FOR COLLEGE, BUT QUITE ANOTHER TO GO SO FAR AWAY TO BE ON SOME REALITY TV SHOW YOU MIGHT NOT WIN.
BUT IT'LL BE JUST LIKE A SCHOOL AND I'LL LEARN **SO MUCH!**
I'LL THINK ABOUT IT.

LET'S ENTER THE COMPETITION, IT'LL BE SO MUCH FUN!
LET'S ENTER THE COMPETITION, IT'LL BE SO MUCH FUN!
SORRY, ROSE, YOU KNOW I CAN'T LEAVE THE RESTAURANT RIGHT NOW!

P.E.I.
POTAT
Batter Royale?
NOPE!

MAYBE WE SHOULD LET HER GO, CASSANDRA!
I KNOW WE DON'T AGREE ON A LOT, BUT IF SHE WANTS TO TRY TO EARN THE TUITION FOR COLLEGE, MAYBE THIS IS HER SHOT.
UGH, FINE!
BUT, I'D RATHER YOU HAVE SOMEONE YOU KNOW AS YOUR TEAMMATE.
I KNOW JUST THE GUY!

I NEED TO TALK TO YOU AT LUNCH.
ME TOO.

HEY!

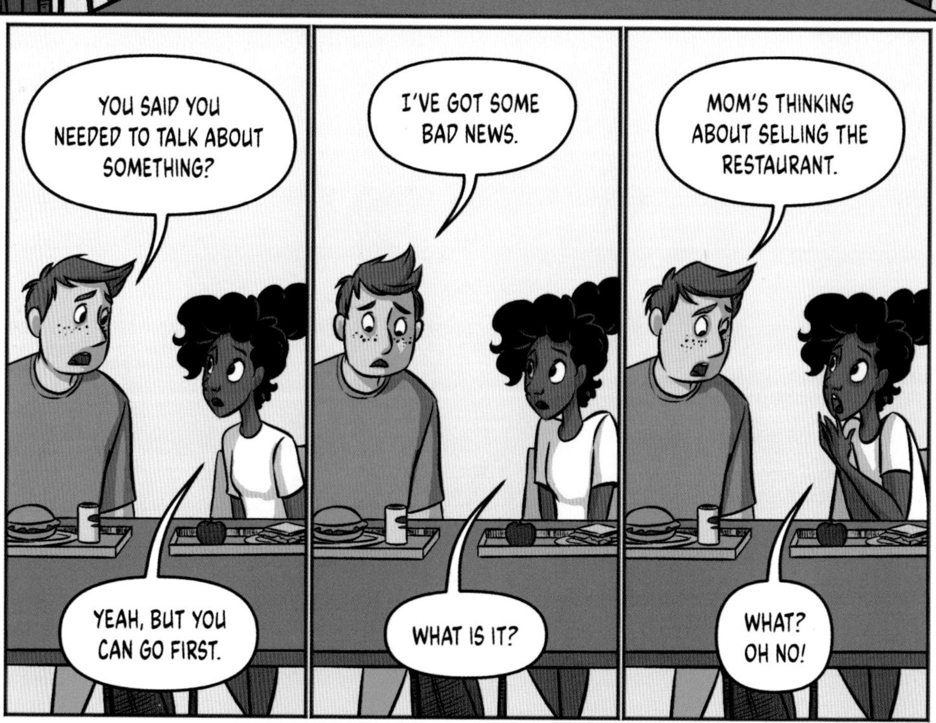
YOU SAID YOU NEEDED TO TALK ABOUT SOMETHING?
YEAH, BUT YOU CAN GO FIRST.
I'VE GOT SOME BAD NEWS.
WHAT IS IT?
MOM'S THINKING ABOUT SELLING THE RESTAURANT.
WHAT? OH NO!

I DON'T FEEL BAD FOR MYSELF, BUT IT'S HER LIFE'S WORK, AND IT'S HORRIBLE FOR EVERYONE WORKING THERE.
FOR SURE . . .
SO, WHAT WAS YOUR THING?
WITH EVERYTHING GOING ON, I FORGOT TO SHOW YOU THIS!
FIELDBERRY CULINARY IN TORONTO!
THAT'S AMAZING!

SO, I GUESS YOU'D BE MOVING AWAY AND ALL THAT?
WELL, THE PROBLEM IS I CAN'T AFFORD THE TUITION.
THAT'S WHY I **NEED** TO WIN THIS CONTEST.
LOOK, YOU'VE ALWAYS WANTED TO TRAVEL. THIS WOULD GIVE YOU THAT CHANCE, *AND* IF THE RESTAURANT GOES UP FOR SALE, MAYBE THIS WILL GIVE US A CHANCE TO SAVE IT. WE WOULD MAKE AN AWESOME TEAM!

THAT MONEY **WOULD** BE A REALLY GREAT BOOST FOR THE RESTAURANT . . . YOU **REALLY** THINK WE CAN DO THIS?
HELL YES!
OKAY . . . I'M IN.
REALLY!?

YES!!!

Directions

1. Preheat oven to 400°F degrees.
2. Whisk together flour, baking powder, salt, and sugar.

3. Cut butter into the flour mixture with a fork until it looks crumbly.

4. Fold in heavy whipping cream.

5 Turn the mixture out onto a floured surface.

6 Shape into a rectangle and fold in blueberries a bit at a time.

7 Once the blueberries are mixed in, roll into a rectangle again and cut into squares or wedges.

8 Place scones on a baking sheet and brush the tops with milk or egg whites, if using.

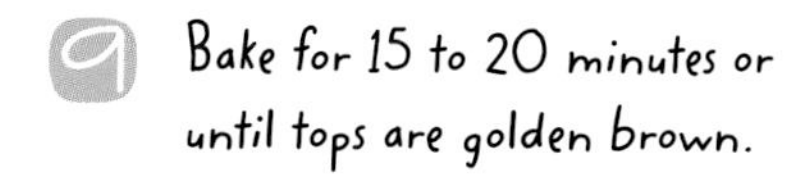

9 Bake for 15 to 20 minutes or until tops are golden brown.

International Arrivals

BATTER ROYALE
WELCOME TO LONDON!
I'M ELISABETH MOODY, PRODUCTION MANAGER FOR *BATTER ROYALE*.
FOLLOW ME.
BATTER ROYALE

EMILY HERE WILL SHOW YOU TO YOUR ROOM. HERE'S MY CARD.
TAPING STARTS TOMORROW MORNING AT 7 A.M. A CAB WILL BE HERE TO TAKE YOU TO THE STUDIO. LOVELY!
CAN I SHOW YOU TO YOUR ROOM?

EACH TEAM HAS A ROOM ON THIS FLOOR, AND A SHARED BATHROOM IS AT THE END OF THE HALL.
HONESTLY, I THOUGHT THEY WOULD'VE PUT YOU IN A FANCIER SPOT.
AT LEAST IT'S COZY.
HERE ARE YOUR KEYS. ANY QUESTIONS, I'M ALWAYS DOWNSTAIRS.

I CALL TOP BUNK!
I THOUGHT . . . WE'D ALL HAVE OUR OWN ROOMS!
WELL, I GUESS IT MAKES SENSE IF EACH TEAM HAS A ROOM . . .
I GUESS . . .
MAYBE WE SHOULD EXPLORE THE CITY?
OF COURSE! WE'RE IN LONDON! WE SHOULD BE OUT AND ABOUT GOING ON ADVENTURES. YOU'RE TOTALLY RIGHT.
ZZZ
ZZZ

I SWEAR IT WASN'T ME.
CREAK
SIGH!

I'VE JUST FOUND THE BEST BATHROOM IN THIS PLACE!
NO FAIR.
IT WAS LIKE A SPA!
UMM, WHAT TIME ARE WE SUPPOSED TO GET TO THE STUDIO?
7:30?
OH NO! WE'RE GONNA BE LATE!
WHAT ABOUT BREAKFAST?
FORGET IT!

Sally's
OPEN
Sally's
MENU

HELLO, AND WELCOME EVERYONE! I'M SALLY SLICE, WORLD-RENOWNED PASTRY CHEF AND HOST OF *BATTER ROYALE!*
PLEASE EVERYONE, HAVE A SWEET—I MEAN, SEAT.
WHERE ARE THE CANADIAN CONTESTANTS?

HERE THEY ARE!

THAT DAMN CABBIE, MAKING THE TWO OF YOU LATE!
PLEASED TO MEET THE BOTH OF YOU!

!
MWAH!

THE TEAMS WILL COMPETE OVER FIVE DAYS . . .
EACH DAY WILL BRING A NEW CHALLENGE AND AN ELIMINATION. AT THE END OF EACH ROUND, I WILL PERSONALLY JUDGE YOUR CREATIONS AND ELIMINATE A TEAM BASED ON THE RESULTS.
THE WINNERS WILL RECEIVE A GRAND PRIZE OF $500,000 AMERICAN DOLLARS AND A DELICIOUS BOOK DEAL!

?
AHEM!
WE'RE HERE TO BAKE, NOT EAT!

THERE WILL BE LOTS OF TWISTS AND SURPRISES THROUGHOUT THE CONTEST, JUST TO KEEP EVERYONE ON THEIR TOES!
NOW . . .
CONTRACT
CLICK!
WHAT'S THIS LINE ABOUT IMMI "NUT" DEATH?
CONTESTANTS—
. . . YOU HAVE **ONE** HOUR TO IMPRESS ME WITH YOUR SIGNATURE DESSERT . . . GO!

OF COURSE, THERE ISN'T ENOUGH FOR EVERYONE, BUT YOU **ARE** ALLOWED TO BORROW ONE THING FROM EACH TEAM. SHARING IS CARING! OF COURSE, THE OTHER TEAM CAN REFUSE OR STRIKE A DEAL. HAPPY BAKING!
FLOUR
SUGAR
AAAH!

OH! I FORGOT TO MENTION, YOU'LL HAVE TO LOOK OUT FOR TRAPS!
WHAT KIND OF CONTEST IS THIS??
WE JUST WANTED TO MAKE DESSERTS!

THEN MAYBE YOU SHOULD'VE STAYED HOME.

SHOOM!
SHOOM!
ROLL
FLOUR
SUGAR
LOOKS LIKE I CAN ALLOW ONE OTHER TEAM TO WALK THROUGH SAFELY. WHO SHOULD I CHOOSE? HMM . . .
I CHOOSE THE CANADIANS. ROSE, IS IT?

NICE WORK, NICOLE!

DO YOU KNOW WHY I CHOSE YOU?
IT'S BECAUSE YOU DON'T STAND A CHANCE, LOSERS.

RIGHT. I'LL GET THE STRAWBERRIES.
FLOUR
SUGAR
SUGAR
COF

60:00

POOF!

FOOM

SPLAT!

WHAT ARE YOU DOING? I THOUGHT WE WERE MAKING THE STRAWBERRY SHORTCAKE?
I THINK WE SHOULD DO SOMETHING NEW, YOU KNOW, TO IMPRESS SALLY!

WHAT? BUT THIS IS WHAT GOT US HERE!
TRUST ME!

48:09

OOOH,
SORRY!

JUST BECAUSE YOU CAN COOK THINGS AT HOME DOESN'T MEAN YOU'RE CUT OUT FOR WORKING IN A REAL KITCHEN.

HI.

ROSE?
OH, THAT LOOKS AMAZING!

HOW DO YOU GET THE PETALS SO THIN?
I USE THIS!

THEY'D BE EVEN BETTER IF I HAD A BIT OF POWDERED SUGAR . . .
OH, WE HAVE SOME!
HEY!
OHMYGOSH! THANK YOU **SO** MUCH!
ROSE, FOCUS! WE'RE RUNNING OUT OF TIME!
DIDN'T WE NEED THAT?

FWOOP!
SPLAT!
WHO THREW THAT?

WHAT DO WE DO?

SPLAT!

SUIT UP?

SPLAT!
STOP!
FLOUR
TIME IS RUNNING OUT, FOLKS!!!

00:00
TIME'S UP!

NUT-TING TO SHOW? SHAME.
UGH, UNDERBAKED!
CRUST IS A BIT SOGGY.
IS THIS REALLY YOUR BEST?
THIS ISN'T BAD ACTUALLY.

TERRIBLE.
TOO DRY.

OH, COME ON!

CONSIDER YOURSELVES LUCKY.

I'M SORRY. YOU'VE BEEN OUT-BAKED!

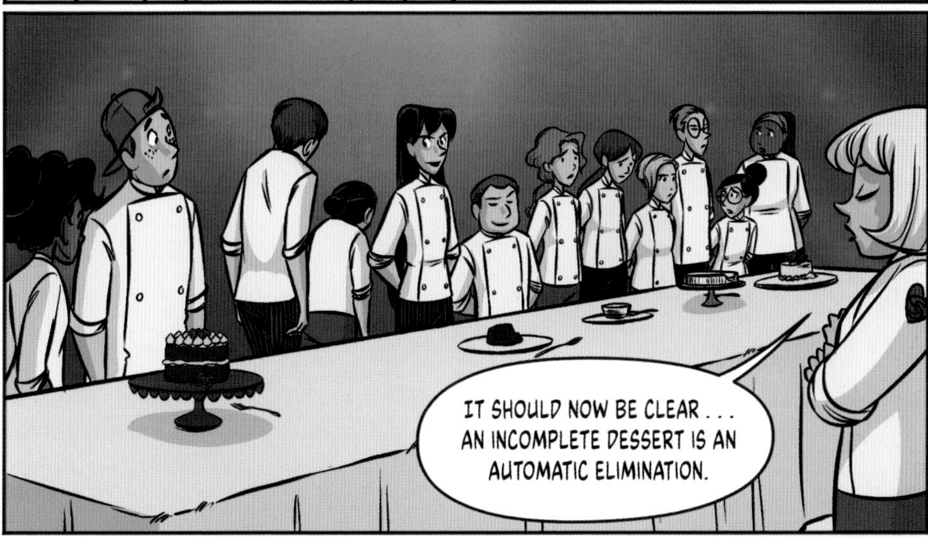
IT SHOULD NOW BE CLEAR . . . AN INCOMPLETE DESSERT IS AN AUTOMATIC ELIMINATION.

NONE OF YOU ARE READY FOR THIS LEVEL OF COMPETITION! ACCORDINGLY, YOU WILL BE GIVEN ONE DAY TO BRUSH UP YOUR SKILLS BEFORE THE NEXT ROUND.
DON'T EVEN DREAM OF DISAPPOINTING ME! SEE YOU IN TWO DAYS!

⅓ cup self-rising flour

½ cup all-purpose flour

½ teaspoon baking soda

⅓ cup cocoa powder

FOR THE Cake

¾ cup softened butter

¾ cup sugar

1 teaspoon vanilla extract

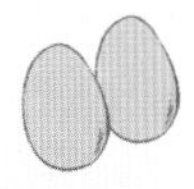

2 eggs

5 ounces buttermilk

Directions

1. Preheat oven to 350ºF. Line a 6-inch cake pan with parchment.
2. Sift the self-rising and all-purpose flours and then combine in a medium bowl.
3. Add the baking soda and cocoa powder, then whisk together and set aside.
4. Cream together butter, sugar, and vanilla until fluffy. Add eggs, one at a time, until well combined.

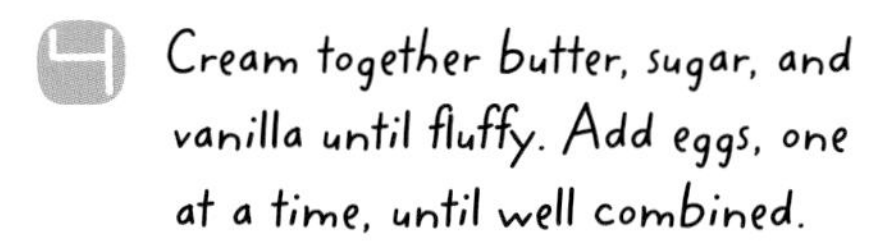

5. Add the dry mix to the wet ingredients alternatively with the buttermilk, stirring until combined.
6. Pour into prepared cake pan. Bake for 50 minutes.

FOR THE Strawberries

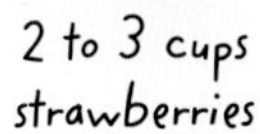

- 2 to 3 cups strawberries

- 4 tablespoons sugar

Directions

1. Remove tops from strawberries and slice (leave 4 or 5 whole). Place into a small bowl and coat with sugar and set aside.

FOR THE Topping

- 1 cup heavy whipping cream

- ½ teaspoon vanilla

- 2 tablespoons powdered sugar

- ½ teaspoon gelatin powder (optional)

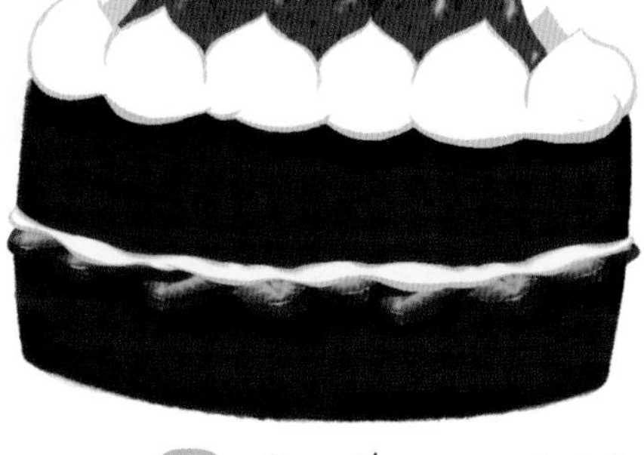

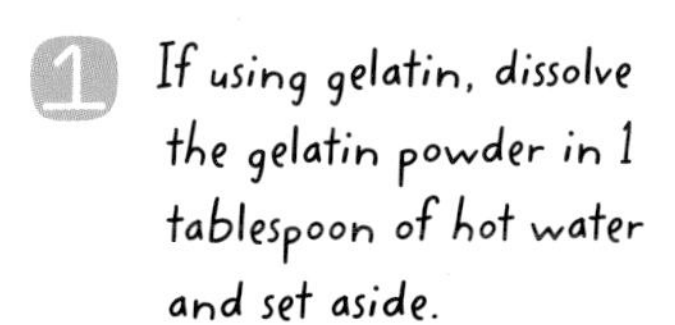

Directions

1. If using gelatin, dissolve the gelatin powder in 1 tablespoon of hot water and set aside.
2. Using a hand blender or mixer with a whisk attachment, beat the heavy whipping cream on low, then slowly turn it up to medium speed. (Add the gelatin mixture as it thickens.)

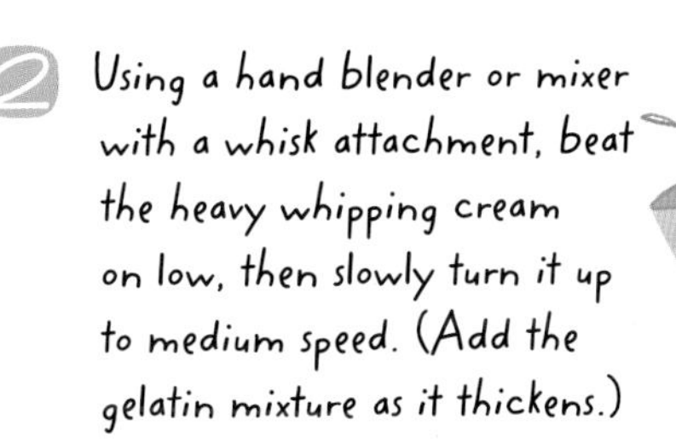

3. Once the cream starts to hold its shape, add the vanilla and powdered sugar. Turn the speed to high and continue to whip until stiff peaks form.

ASSEMBLY

When your cake is fully cooled, slice into two equal layers. On your bottom layer, spread a thin layer of whipped cream, then add cut strawberries and piped whipped cream on top. Place the other cake layer on top and repeat the layers of whipped cream and strawberries. Place whole strawberries on top.

TIPS

- Drizzle with melted chocolate or top with chocolate flakes.

SO, ABOUT THE BOOBY TRAPS AT THE BEGINNING . . .
I DON'T REMEMBER DARLA TELLING US ANYTHING ABOUT THAT.
THIS IS WAY MORE INTENSE THAN I THOUGHT IT WOULD BE.
THE NEXT ROUND IS TOMORROW! WHAT ARE WE GONNA DO?
WE CAN'T FREAK OUT. WE JUST NEED TO PRACTICE. WE CAN DO THIS . . .
RIGHT?
UMM, ER . . .YEAH, I THINK SO.

HEY!
HEY!
HEY!

SO, YOU'RE CANADIAN THEN?
IS THAT THE SAME AS BEING AMERICAN?
UMM . . . NO.

I'M LILY, FROM JAPAN.
CLARA AND I HAVE BEEN ONLINE FRIENDS SINCE FOREVER!
I'M CLARA, FROM HERE IN LONDON!
THIS COMPETITION WAS THE PERFECT CHANCE TO GET TOGETHER!

SO OUT OF THEIR LEAGUE . . .
THOSE TWO ARE LUCAS AND NICOLE. THEY'RE SERIOUS PROFESSIONALS.
I DON'T THINK SHE'S EVER LOST A COMPETITION IN HER LIFE!
HER FATHER OWNS A RESTAURANT IN PARIS, SO SHE HAS TO LIVE UP TO HIS REPUTATION.
I KINDA KNOW WHAT THAT'S LIKE . . .

NEXT DAY
9:00
BEEP BEEP BEEP
C'MON! WE'VE GOTTA GET GOING IF WE WANT TO GET IN SOME PRACTICE!
UGH, I DUNNO IF I CAN MAKE IT TODAY . . .
SERIOUSLY? WE CAN'T DROP OUT BECAUSE OF A COLD! LET'S GO FIND SOME MEDS.

HEY, CAN YOU DIRECT US TO THE NEAREST, YA KNOW, PHARMACY OR SOMEPLACE, FOR COLD MEDICINE?
PHARMACY? FOLLOW ME.
WE'VE GOT WHATEVER YOU NEED RIGHT HERE!

TEST KITCHEN
SORRY, THIS SPACE IS OCCUPIED!
WHAT?
YOU SNOOZE YOU LOSE.
BUT **YOU** CAN STAY IF YOU WANT.
HELL NO, BUDDY.
WE'LL FIND SOMEPLACE ELSE.

WHAT DO WE DO NOW?
WE NEED TO PRACTICE!
FOLLOW ME!
NICE OF EMILY TO HOOK US UP WITH THE HOSTEL KITCHEN!
YEAH!
YOU BETTER MAKE ME SOMETHING DELICIOUS!
LET'S GET STARTED!

SERIOUSLY THOUGH, WHAT CHANCE DO WE HAVE AGAINST EVERYONE WHEN THEY'VE ALL GOT CRAZY NINJA SKILLS?
I THOUGHT WE DID OKAY.
WE NEED EVERYTHING TO BE PRECISE, AS WELL AS ORIGINAL . . . SOMETHING THAT SAYS "US."
I MEAN, NOT US AS IN "US" BUT, US LIKE WHERE WE'RE FROM . . . US.
MAPLE . . .
MAPLE SYRUP
HOW ABOUT MAPLE INFUSED CHOCOLATE?
HMM . . .
AND BACON?
IT SCREAMS CANADA.
WE JUST NEED AN ORIGINAL WAY TO PUT IT TOGETHER . . .

MAPLE
CHOCOLATE
CRUMBS
SUGAR
I DON'T KNOW IF PUTTING THE MAPLE INTO THE CHOCOLATE MAKES IT TOO SWEET? YOU'LL HAVE TO TRY SOME.
I CAN'T GET A SPOON—MY HANDS ARE A MESS!
TRY.

IT'S
GOOD . . .
I LIKE IT.

COMING UP! THESE FIVE TEAMS WILL BATTLE IT OUT FOR THE TITLE OF BEST DESSERT CHEF . . .
. . . A BOOK DEAL, AND CASH PRIZE OF FIVE HUNDRED THOUSAND DOLLARS!

I AM YOUR HOST!
WORLD RENOWNED PASTRY CHEF, SALLY SLICE!
ONLY THE CREAM OF THE CROP, WILL RISE TO THE TOP!
Batter Royale

FOR THIS ROUND, YOU ARE REQUIRED TO MAKE AN ORIGINAL DESSERT!
THERE'S JUST ONE CATCH.
YOU'LL NEVER *BAKE* THESE CHAINS!
SNAP!
WHAT??
AAAAND GO!

I REALLY WANT YOUR DESSERT TO BE AMAZING. MAKE ME FEEL SOMETHING!

OK, LET'S GO!

WE HAVE TO MOVE TOGETHER OR WE WON'T GET THROUGH THIS ROUND!
WHUMP!

SURPRISE INGREDIENT, LADIES AND GENTS!
BRUSSELS SPROUTS!
MAKE YOUR WAY OVER! AND DON'T FORGET, THIS INGREDIENT **MUST** BE FULLY INCORPORATED INTO YOUR CREATION!

WHAT THE HELL ARE WE GONNA DO WITH BRUSSELS SPROUTS?
I DUNNO . . .
MAYBE IF WE PUT IT INTO THE CRUST, IT'LL DISGUISE THE TASTE?

THAT COULD WORK.

NOW **THAT** IS A GREAT IDEA!

SO ROSE, WHAT'S IT LIKE WHERE YOU'RE FROM? COLD?

NO, NOT ALL THE TIME . . .

WELL, IT WAS NICE CHATTING WITH YOU!
WHIRRR

FILLING IS DONE!
CRUST TOO!
GAG
MORE SUGAR SHOULD FIX IT!

HMM, NOT BAD!

I . . . DON'T UNDERSTAND, WE'VE DONE THIS RECIPE A MILLION TIMES!

I ONLY ADDED THE SPROUTS AS GARNISH. THE TASTE SHOULD BE THE SAME!
YOU SHOULD BE TASTING EVERYTHING, EVEN IF YOU'VE DONE IT A MILLION TIMES.

I'M SORRY, YOU'VE BEEN OUT-BAKED.

THIS COMPETITION IS TOUGHER THAN I THOUGHT . . .

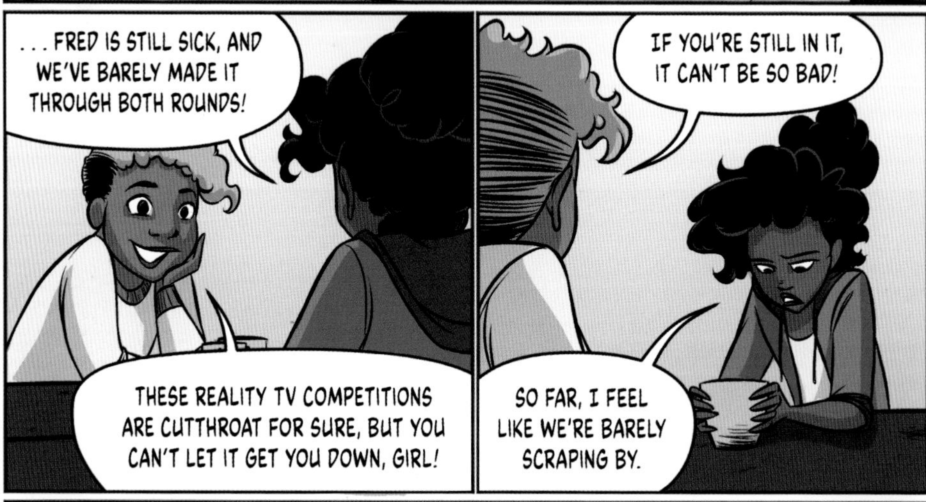
. . . FRED IS STILL SICK, AND WE'VE BARELY MADE IT THROUGH BOTH ROUNDS!
THESE REALITY TV COMPETITIONS ARE CUTTHROAT FOR SURE, BUT YOU CAN'T LET IT GET YOU DOWN, GIRL!
IF YOU'RE STILL IN IT, IT CAN'T BE SO BAD!
SO FAR, I FEEL LIKE WE'RE BARELY SCRAPING BY.
THANKS FOR THE CHAT, EMILY!

HEY! ROSE, STILL IN THE COMPETITION! I GUESS I CAN'T BE SURPRISED, SINCE YOU HAVE A PARTNER WHO ACTUALLY KNOWS HOW TO COOK.
I THINK THE ONLY COMPETITION YOU'LL BE WINNING AT THIS RATE IS FOR MOST INSUFFERABLE KNOW-IT-ALL.
ROSE?
EVERYTHING OK?
HEY, FRED! NICE JOB IN THERE TODAY!
YEAH, UM, THANKS. WHAT'S YOUR DEAL ANYWAY?

MY DEAL? MY DEAL IS THAT THIS CONTEST IS SUPPOSED TO BE FOR PROFESSIONALS LIKE US . . .
. . . NOT AMATEURS LIKE HER.
WELL AT THIS POINT, IT LOOKS LIKE YOU MIGHT JUST GET BEATEN BY AN AMATEUR.
. . .
LET'S GO.
I'LL BE RIGHT BACK.

WHY ARE YOU TREATING ROSE LIKE THIS?
YOUR MOM OWNS A RESTAURANT, RIGHT?
YEAH.
SO, YOU GET THAT I HAVE MY DAD'S REPUTATION TO LIVE UP TO.
SURE.
SO WHY WOULD I WANT TO COMPETE AGAINST SOMEONE WITH ZERO EXPERIENCE? I MEAN, SHE CAN'T EVEN CRACK AN EGG PROPERLY.
AND DESPITE ALL THAT SHE'S STILL IN THE COMPETITION. MAYBE SHE'S BETTER THAN YOU THINK?
PFFT! YEAH, WE'LL SEE.

ROSE MAY BE NEW TO THIS, BUT I WOULDN'T UNDERESTIMATE HER IF I WERE YOU.
OH YEAH? WHAT'S SO SPECIAL ABOUT HER?
SHE'S GOT AN AMAZING RAW TALENT! SHE CAN COME UP WITH RECIPES IN HER HEAD, ON THE SPOT. SHE HAS A GREAT SENSE OF WHAT FLAVORS GO TOGETHER. SHE'S JUST AS WORTHY A COMPETITOR AS ANY OF US!
NOT TO MENTION, SHE WORKS REALLY WELL WITH OTHERS IN THE KITCHEN, WHICH I'M NOT SURE I CAN SAY FOR YOU.
CLEARLY IT'S HARD FOR YOU TO BE OBJECTIVE BECAUSE YOU OBVIOUSLY LIKE HER.
WE'RE JUST FRIENDS.

OH YEAH? I BET SHE'S THRILLED YOU'RE OUT HERE WITH ME INSTEAD OF WITH HER RIGHT NOW.

Maple Chocolate Cream Cheese Tart

Makes one 4-inch tart

For the Crust

½ cup chocolate baking crumbs

3 tablespoons melted butter

Directions

1. Combine ingredients and pour into a 4-inch pan.

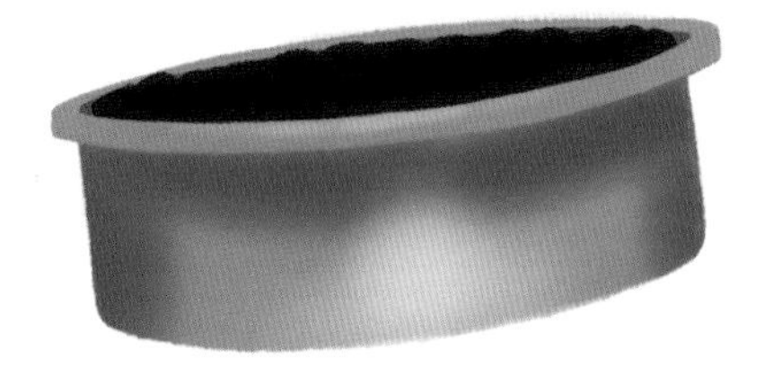

2. Use the bottom of a glass to press crust evenly to the bottom and up the sides.
3. Chill in the refrigerator while you make your filling.

1 tablespoon maple syrup

⅓ cup heavy whipping cream

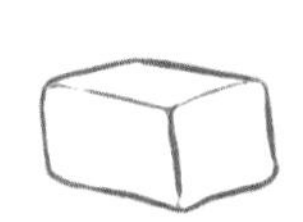

½ cup cream cheese

¼ cup icing sugar

For the Filling

Directions

1. Using a hand mixer or stand mixer with a whisk attachment, whisk ingredients together until well blended.

Chocolate Maple — For the Glaze

1/4 cup maple syrup

1/8 cup cocoa powder

Directions

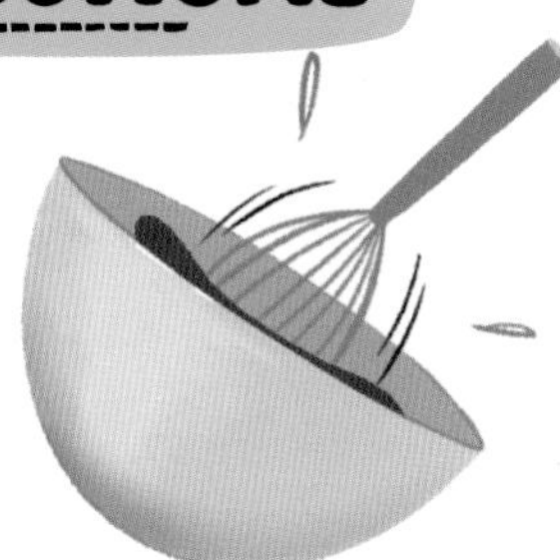

1. Combine ingredients in a small bowl.
2. Mix ingredients together until well blended. You can adjust the amount of cocoa or maple syrup depending on your taste.

ASSEMBLY

Using a piping bag, pipe the filling onto the chocolate crust. Drizzle maple glaze on top.

- Top with bacon crumble or a bacon slice!

TIPS

MUST BE HAVING A SHOWER.
HAVE YOU SEEN FRED AROUND? WE'LL BE LATE FOR THE NEXT ROUND!
HE SAID HE WANTED TO HEAD IN EARLY AND HE'D MEET YOU THERE.
O-KAY.

SOMEONE FROM EVERY TEAM IS MISSING!
I HAVE NO IDEA WHAT'S GOING ON.
WHAT?
MAYBE THIS IS ALL PART OF ANOTHER CHALLENGE.
WOULD SALLY REALLY DO THAT?

Batter Royale
HEY! WHAT IS THIS?
GOOD MORNING, CONTESTANTS! TODAY WE HAVE A BERRY SPECIAL CHALLENGE!

YOUR PARTNERS ARE ALL TIED IN THE CENTER, EACH WITH THEIR OWN LOCK.
FINISH THE RECIPE I PROVIDE **EXACTLY** AS IT'S WRITTEN, AND YOU WILL EARN THE KEY TO THEIR ESCAPE.
THE LAST ONE TO FINISH IS OUT OF THE COMPETITION. QUICKLY NOW, GET TO YOUR TABLES!

OKAY, I NEED TWO CUPS OF ALMOND FLOUR. GOT IT. EGG WHITES, CHECK.

ICING SUGAR

AAAAAH!
ICING SUGAR

I GOT SOME LEMON IN MY EYES!

OVER HERE!
THERE.

YOU OKAY?
YEAH.
THANK YOU!
NO
PROBLEM!

Batter Royale

MFFMM!

SORRY YOU TWO!
YOU'VE BEEN OUT-BAKED!
ROSE!
WE ALMOST LOST!
YOU REALLY NEED TO
FOCUS NEXT ROUND.
LILY GOT LEMON IN HER
EYES AND NEEDED HELP!
I COULDN'T JUST
IGNORE HER!

WHAT'S THE BIG DEAL? WE'VE MADE IT THIS FAR!
WE'VE COME IN ALMOST LAST EVERY TIME!
I ADMIT AT THE START WE WERE OUT OF SYNC, AND I WAS UNSURE, BUT I THINK WE'RE GETTING BETTER!
WE WERE THIS CLOSE TO BEING ELIMINATED **AGAIN** TODAY. ALL BECAUSE **YOU** KEEP GETTING DISTRACTED.

OKAY, I ADMIT I WAS WASN'T PAYING ATTENTION A COUPLE OF TIMES, BUT—
THERE'S NO ROOM FOR DISTRACTION!
IF A FRIEND **SERIOUSLY** NEEDS HELP, I HAVE TO DO SOMETHING!
THE ONLY THING YOU SHOULD BE **SERIOUS** ABOUT RIGHT NOW IS WINNING.
YOU NEED TO BE CUTTHROAT! WE CAN'T AFFORD ANY MISTAKES!
THAT'S ASSUMING YOU REALLY WANT TO WIN.

OF COURSE I WANT TO WIN. BUT I DON'T WANT TO BE RUTHLESS IN ORDER TO GET THERE. I'M NOT NICOLE.
THEN . . . MAYBE THIS WAS ALL A MISTAKE.
IF WE'RE NOT IN IT TO WIN, WE MIGHT AS WELL GO HOME.
I WON'T GIVE UP NOW.

I MAY NOT BE THE BEST AT THIS, I MAY NOT BE THE FIERCEST COMPETITOR, BUT I'M **NOT** A QUITTER.
I NEED YOU TO BELIEVE THAT WE CAN DO THIS.
I DO . . .
I JUST FEEL LIKE A LOT IS RIDING ON THIS WIN. THE RESTAURANT, YOU GOING TO SCHOOL . . .
I KNOW. I FEEL IT TOO.
WE *NEED* TO WIN. OR ALL THIS IS FOR NOTHING.

Macarons

MAKES SHELLS FOR 15 to 20 MACARONS

1 ½ cups icing sugar

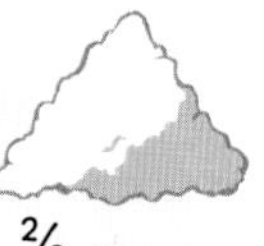

⅔ cup almond flour

3 egg whites

3 tablespoons sugar

icing, ganache, or lemon curd (for filling)

Directions

1. Preheat oven to 325°F. Blend icing sugar and almond flour in a food processor and set aside.

2. With a hand mixer or stand mixer with a whisk attachment, whisk the egg whites until foamy. Add 1 tablespoon of sugar at a time, whisking until incorporated. Keep whisking until the egg whites get stiff and glossy.

3. Fold the almond flour mixture into the egg whites. The mixture should look smooth.

4. Fill a piping bag with the batter (I use a Wilton #12 tip) and pipe small rounds of batter onto a lined baking sheet.

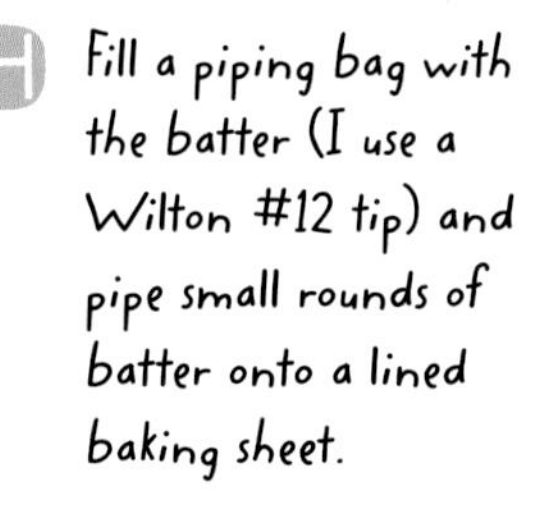

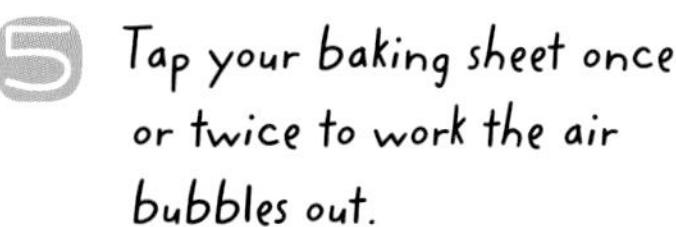

5. Tap your baking sheet once or twice to work the air bubbles out.

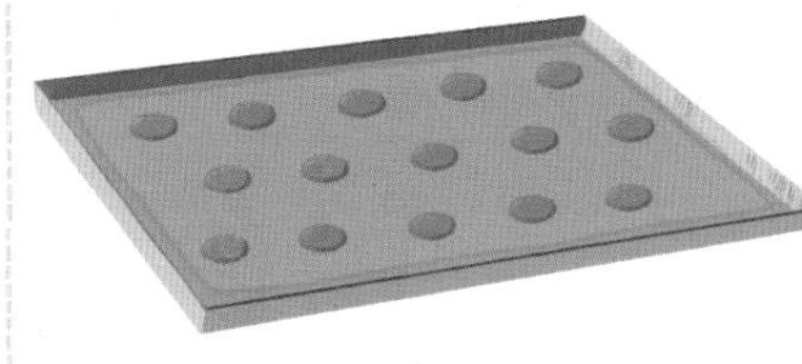

6. Leave the cookies to dry for about 15 minutes. You can make sure they are dry enough by gently touching the surface. If your finger comes away clean, they're dry enough. The drier the better. Bake for 10 minutes.

7. Once fully cooled, spread half the cookies with icing, ganache, or lemon curd and top with the remaining cookies!

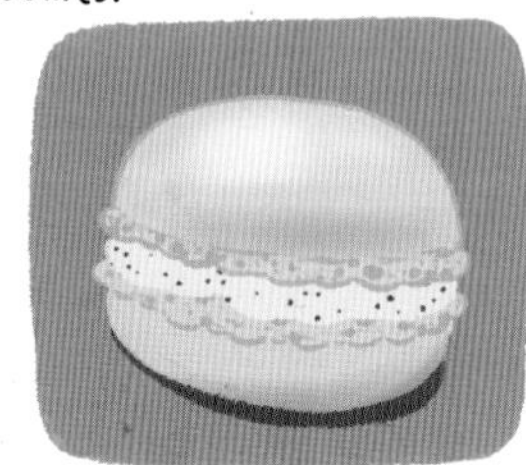

FLOWER MARKET
FLOWER MARKET

WELCOME, MY PRETTY PETALS, TO THE COVENT GARDEN FLOWER MARKET!
EACH TEAM HAS BEEN GIVEN A TYPE OF FLOWER THEY NEED TO FIND. THESE FLOWERS WILL BE THE DECORATION FOR YOUR CAKE IN THE NEXT PART OF THE ROUND.
YOU MUST RACE THROUGH THE MARKET, FIND YOUR FLOWERS, PUT PETAL TO THE METAL, AND MAKE IT BACK HERE TO THE FINISH LINE!

FIRST TEAM TO WIN GETS SWEET BONUS TIME FOR THE NEXT ROUND, PLUS A SPECIAL EVENING RIDE ON THE LONDON EYE!
ON YOUR MARK! GET SET! **GO!**

PINK PEONY

SO, YOU LIKE TO TRAVEL? MAYBE YOU CAN VISIT ME IN PARIS SOMETIME. YOU KNOW, AFTER THE COMPETITION IS OVER?
UMM, WELL . . .
I GOT OUR FLOWER.

CONGRATULATIONS! YOU ARE THE FIRST TO MAKE IT BACK! ROSE AND FRED WIN THE ROUND!

YOU TRULY **ROSE** TO THE OCCASION! HAVE A DELICIOUS TIME ON THE LONDON EYE!

WOW, THIS IS AMAZING!
MUNCH! MUNCH!
DO YOU THINK WE COULD ACTUALLY WIN THIS THING?
WHY SO SAD? WE WON THE ROUND.
WE ONLY WON BECAUSE I MADE IT TO THE FINISH LINE, WHILE YOU WERE BUSY CHATTING IT UP WITH NICOLE.

SHE'S ACTUALLY NOT AS MEAN AS YOU THINK, ONCE YOU GET TO KNOW HER . . . WELL . . . KINDA.
WAIT, ARE YOU JEALOUS?
HELL NO!
HEY, I'VE BEEN SERIOUS ABOUT WINNING THIS! YOU SAID YOU WERE TOO.
IT'S NOT *JUST* ABOUT THAT. . .
THEN WHY ARE YOU UPSET?
I GUESS, I'M UPSET ABOUT MY PARENTS SPLITTING UP. MAYBE I COULD'VE DONE MORE.

IT'S NOT YOUR FAULT.

I KNOW WE'VE BEEN FRIENDS SINCE FOREVER BUT . . . THE OTHER NIGHT WHEN WERE IN THE KITCHEN . . . I THOUGHT I FELT . . . MORE.

AM I WRONG? I MEAN, DO YOU LIKE NICOLE? JUST LET ME KNOW AND WE CAN FORGET IT.

I DON'T LIKE NICOLE.
IT'S REALLY NONE OF MY BUSINESS.
I LIKE YOU.
OH.

EVER SINCE WE WERE KIDS. THAT HASN'T CHANGED.

SO, NOW WHAT DO WE DO?
DO WE WANT TO RUIN OUR FRIENDSHIP?

I THINK WE'VE ALREADY RUINED IT.

WHAT?
MY NOSE IS RUNNING ISN'T IT.
YEAH!
UGH, IS THIS ALL ON CAMERA?
PROBABLY!

Batter Royale
HEY, WHAT'S THAT?
THIS SOURDOUGH STARTER IS TWO HUNDRED YEARS OLD. USE IT IN THE NEXT CHALLENGE. —SALLY
WHAT THE HECK CAN WE DO WITH TWO-HUNDRED-YEAR OLD SOURDOUGH STARTER?
FRED?
WHAT'S WRONG?
UH. . . I THINK I ATE TOO MUCH!

DON'T WORRY, WE'RE ALMOST DOWN!

THIS WAS REALLY KINDA NIC—
FRED?

C'MON!
WHAT'S GOING ON?
DO YOU SEE ANY CAMERAS?
NO.
GOOD.
LET'S GO GET MILKSHAKES!

I WANT TO WIN THIS. I WANT YOUR MOM TO GET HER RESTAURANT BACK, AND ME TO EARN MY DEGREE,
AND I WANT TO PROVE A COUPLE OF **AMATEURS** CAN DO THIS.
WE WILL. I BELIEVE IN US.
YOU KNOW, I'M ACTUALLY LOOKING FORWARD TO THE NEXT ROUND.
202
202

OH YEAH, WE'RE BOTH IN THE SAME ROOM.
NOT AWKWARD AT ALL NOW.

UMM, I'LL LET YOU DO YOUR THING, AND COME BACK LATER, OKAY?
YEAH, OKAY THANKS.

I HAD A REALLY GREAT TIME.

ARE THERE ANY CAMERAS?

GOOD NIGHT.
202

120 grams flour (use any kind but keep it consistent)

120 grams filtered water

Sourdough starter can be made in many different ways, but for this one you use equal weights of flour and water.

Directions

1. Stir flour and water together in a glass jar or bowl. Cover loosely and keep at room temperature or in an oven with the light on (don't forget that it's in there, like I did >.<).

2. Feed it once every twenty-four hours by discarding half of your mixture (120 grams) and adding a fresh 60 grams of flour and 60 grams of water.

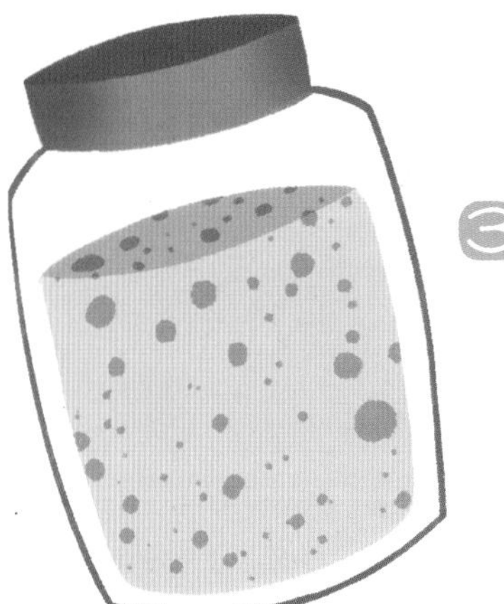

3. After several days, the mixture should bubble and rise. Then you can feed it twice a day, every twelve hours. It may take several days or weeks of feeding before it's ready to use. You will know it is ready when it becomes very bubbly, with a dramatic rise in volume.

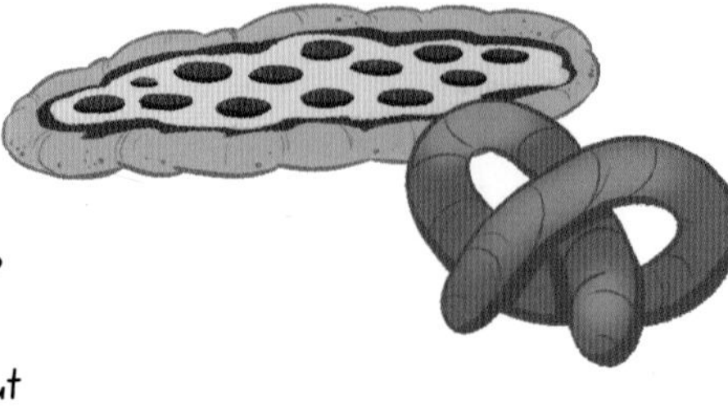

- You don't need to throw away the discarded starter! Keep it separately to use for pancakes, pizza crust, pretzels, and more! There are tons of recipes out there for sourdough discard!

ORCHID
PEONY
HYDRANGEA

WHEN YOUR DESIGNS ARE DONE, YOU WILL NEED TO RACE TO GATHER YOUR INGREDIENTS.
YOU MAY FIND THEIR LOCATION A BIT **SIZZLING**!

SERIOUSLY?

DAMN!

FLOUR
EXCELLENT! NOW YOU HAVE A CHOICE . . .
PUSH THE SWITCH, AND CLOSE THE PIT SO EVERYONE CAN WALK THROUGH FREELY—

—OR MAKE THE NEXT TEAM EARN THEIR ACCESS BY USING THE ROPE.

THANKS!

SMASH!
SLAM!
I GOT SOME SELF-RISING FLOUR, BUT NO BUTTER OR SUGAR. WHAT CAN WE DO?

WE'LL HAVE TO BARGAIN WITH SOMEONE.
THERE'S NO WAY I'M BARGAINING WITH MISTY.
HEY GUYS, WHAT'LL IT TAKE TO SCORE SOME BUTTER AND SUGAR?
WHADDAYA GOT?
HOW ABOUT SOME TWO-HUNDRED-YEAR-OLD SOURDOUGH?

SURE, SEND IT OVER!
ZIP
ARE YOU SURE THIS IS A GOOD IDEA?
IT'S GETTING US WHAT WE NEED!
THIS STUFF IS GOLD!
SUGAR

GREAT WORK TEAMS! WE'LL CONTINUE TOMORROW, WITH THE FINISHING OF OUR CAKES AND THE OFFICIAL TASTE TEST!

THE NEXT DAY:
GASP!
WHO WOULD DO THIS!
ALL RIGHT! WHO IS IT?
YOU! YOU DID THIS!
I WOULD NEVER—

AAAAAGH!

WHOA!
THERE'S NO WAY WE'LL WIN THIS ROUND NOW.
NICOLE MUST'VE DONE THIS TOO.
NOW **YOU'RE** BLAMING ME?
YOU'RE THE ONLY ONE WHO DOESN'T SEEM TO HAVE ANYTHING DESTROYED! COINCIDENCE?
TAKE YOUR SOURDOUGH STARTER BACK.
WHAT?

OUR FLOWERS ARE GONE. THERE'S NO WAY WE'LL WIN THIS ROUND NOW. YOU STILL HAVE A CHANCE. USE IT WELL.
HOW SHOULD WE USE IT?
PEONIES
MAPLE CARAMEL
APPLE CRUMBLE
YEAST BASED CAKE
WELL . . . WE WOULDN'T BE HERE IF YOU DIDN'T COME UP WITH THAT DESSERT BACK AT THE RESTAURANT. LET'S DO IT.

02:30
NICOLE AND LUCAS, YOUR CAKE LOOKS AND TASTES EXTRAORDINARY. YOU ARE THE CLEAR WINNERS BY A MILE.
CONGRATULATIONS!

ROSE AND FRED, YOUR CAKE WAS MYSTERIOUSLY DESTROYED, BUT YOU WERE ABLE TO RECOVER YOURSELVES.
YOUR FINAL CAKE ISN'T THE MOST IDEAL IN TERMS OF LOOKS, BUT IT'S THE MOST INVENTIVE CREATION I'VE SEEN SO FAR, AND THE TASTE . . .
WAS ABSOLUTELY DIVINE!
YOU ARE MOVING ON TO THE FINAL ROUND, CONGRATULATIONS!

THIS CAKE IS LACKING IN FLOWERS. WHAT A SHAME!

YOU KNOW WHAT THIS MEANS . . .

YOU'VE BEEN **OUT-BAKED!**

YEAST-BASED Cake

MAKES ONE 9-INCH CAKE

FOR THE Cake

- 2 ¼ teaspoons yeast (or 1 cup sourdough starter)
- ¼ cup sugar
- 2 cups flour (1 cup flour if using sourdough starter)

- ½ teaspoon salt

- ½ cup warm milk

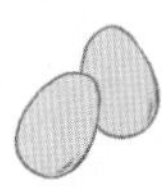

- 2 eggs

- 4 tablespoons melted butter

Directions

1. Preheat oven to 400ºF.
2. (If using yeast) Combine yeast with 1 teaspoon of sugar and ¼ cup of warm water and let stand for about 10 minutes.
3. In a separate bowl, combine flour, remaining sugar, and salt. Add yeast (or starter), milk, and eggs, and beat until combined.

4. Add butter and beat until smooth.
5. Scrape down the sides of the bowl, cover, and let rise until doubled in size (approximately 45 minutes).
6. While the dough is rising, line a 9-inch cake pan with parchment paper.

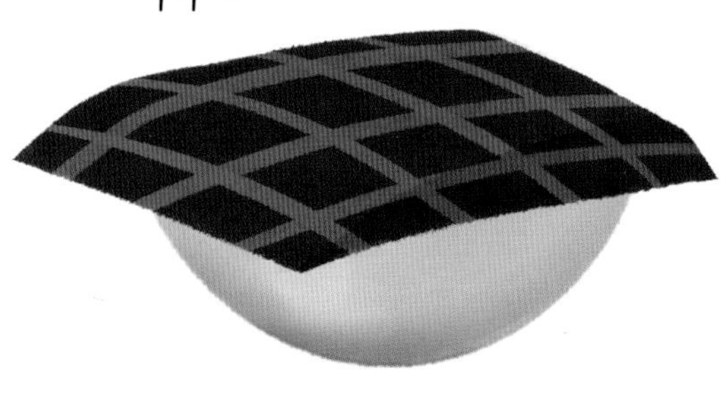

FOR THE Topping

¼ cup sugar

1 teaspoon cinnamon

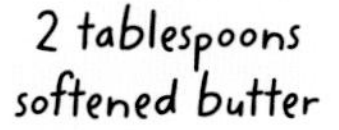

2 tablespoons softened butter

Directions

1. In a small bowl, combine the ¼ cup of sugar and 1 teaspoon of cinnamon and mix.
2. Once risen, place the dough into the prepared cake pan and flatten down evenly. Spread the softened butter on the top, then sprinkle with the combined sugar and cinnamon.
3. Let rise for 15 more minutes. Bake for 25 minutes.

FOR THE Icing

2 cups sugar

2 tablespoons melted butter

1 teaspoon vanilla

2 tablespoons milk

Directions

1. In a medium bowl, combine the ingredients for icing, mix until smooth, and drizzle on top while cake is still warm.

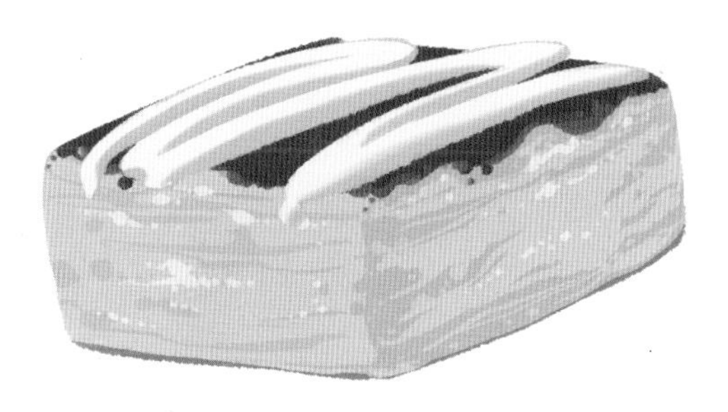

THE NEXT DAY, THE FINAL ROUND APPROACHES . . .
BEFORE WE BEGIN, I HAVE A FEW MORE SURPRISES FOR EACH TEAM.
FAMILY MEMBERS HAVE BEEN FLOWN IN TO ASSIST THE CONTESTANTS IN THE KITCHENS!

HEY, MOM!
HEY, DAD!
ROSE!
HEY!

I CAN'T BELIEVE YOU **BOTH** MADE IT!
ANYTHING FOR YOU, HONEY!

OH, I'VE MISSED YOU SO MUCH! HOW ARE YOU DOING? ARE YOU EATING ENOUGH? NOT JUST CAKE? STAYING OUT OF TROUBLE?
I'M GOOD, MOM. REALLY GOOD.

I'M SURPRISED YOU COULD MAKE IT!
OF COURSE I'LL HELP MY BABY COOK ON INTERNATIONAL TV!
I THOUGHT THIS CONTEST WOULD BE A WASTE OF TIME, BUT YOU SEEM TO BE DOING WELL.
I'M GOING TO WIN THIS.
AGAINST THOSE TWO, YOU'D BETTER!
AHEM.

I'M ALSO EGG-CITED TO ANNOUNCE OUR SPECIAL GUESTS . . .
. . . REPRESENTATIVES FROM FIELDBERRY CULINARY SCHOOL.
NO PRESSURE.
OKAY, BACK TO YOUR STATIONS, TEAMS!

THE FINAL CHALLENGE IS SIMPLE. CREATE A DESSERT TABLE. THE THEME IS A BIRTHDAY PARTY!
ANOTHER TWIST?

ALL FORMER CONTESTANTS ARE BACK!

I HAVE ALREADY CHOSEN WHICH SIDES THEY WILL BE ON, SO YOU'D BUTTER GET RIGHT TO IT THEN!

I'M SO HAPPY YOU MADE IT!

WE **CANNOT** LET HER WIN.

YOU HAVE FIVE HOURS.

BAKE ME PROUD!

OKAY, EVERYONE! ROSE IS TAKING THE LEAD, SO LISTEN UP!

UMM . . . OKAY SO, WE'LL NEED A CAKE . . .

CREAM PUFFS, OH, AND SOME CAKE POPS MAYBE?

I DUNNO, WHAT DO YOU GUYS THINK?

MAYBE WE COULD START SETTING THE TABLE?

SURE!
WE CAN START ON SOME FLOWERS FOR A CAKE, I GUESS?

OKAY.
SHOULD WE HAVE SOME KIND OF THEME?
PROBABLY?

ONCE, I DID A PARTY TABLE WITH A *TITANIC* ZOMBIE THEME! HOW ABOUT WE DO THAT?
WE COULD DO LITTLE ZOMBIE SCULPTURES OUT OF FONDANT AND EYEBALLS ON SOME CUPCAKES AND—
WASN'T THAT FOR MY TENTH BIRTHDAY?
I THINK WE NEED SOMETHING A BIT MORE . . . SOPHISTICATED . . .
AND WE DON'T WANT TO GO TOO CRAZY, IT NEEDS TO BE SOMEWHAT SIMPLE.
YOU CAN'T JUST PUT EVERYTHING OUT WILLY-NILLY! YOU WANT TO GIVE THE TABLE SOME HEIGHT!
BUT THESE PLATES LOOK NICER OVER HERE . . .

YOU CAN NEVER JUST LISTEN TO ME; YOU ALWAYS HAVE TO ARGUE ABOUT EVERYTHING!
HOW'S EVERYTHING GOING?
UMM . . .
WELL, IT'S HARD TO DECIDE WHERE EVERYTHING SHOULD GO . . .
OKAY, JUST WORRY ABOUT PICKING OUT THE DECORATIONS FOR NOW.
OH, GREAT IDEA!

MADISON! DON'T BE AN IDIOT! I NEEDED THAT ICING DONE **YESTERDAY!**
YES, CHEF . . .

IF YOU'RE MAKING CREAM PUFFS, THEY'VE GOT TO BE DONE RIGHT . . .
CRASH
UH, SORRY!
WAIT, MOM,
WAIT!
SIGH

MOM, YOU **NEED** TO LET ROSE AND ME BE IN CHARGE OF THIS!
OKAY THEN, JUST TELL ME WHAT TO DO.

HOLD ON . . .
WE **NEED** TO TALK!

I DON'T KNOW WHAT TO DO NOW! WHEN IT'S JUST YOU AND ME IT'S FINE, BUT . . . A WHOLE TEAM?

I THINK THIS IS YOUR THING.
WHAT DO YOU MEAN "MY THING"?
I THINK YOU'RE A LEADER. I CAN COOK, BUT THERE'S MORE TO RUNNING A KITCHEN. YOU'RE SO GOOD AT ENCOURAGING PEOPLE AND FINDING THEIR STRENGTHS. I THINK YOU GOT THIS!
THANKS.
OKAY, LISTEN UP!
YES, CHEF!

LILY AND CLARA, I WANT YOU TWO ON THE CREAM PUFFS!
YES, CHEF!
YOU TWO ARE ON CAKE POPS!
YES, CHEF!
I WANT YOU TWO TO THINK, "OUTDOOR WOODSY THEME." WE'LL NEED PLATES, A FEW WOODEN CAKE STANDS, GREEN RIBBONS, CANDLES, AND ANYTHING ELSE YOU CAN FIND. CAN I TRUST YOU TWO?
YES, CHEF!
YES, CHEF!
YOU TWO ARE ON CAKE DUTY, SOMETHING RUSTIC.
I KNOW YOU TWO CAN WHIP SOMETHING UP FAST!
YES, CHEF!

00:00
AAAAND TIME'S UP!

LOOKS LIKE YOU'VE BOTH DONE AMAZING WORK. I'M SIMPLY **MELTING**!

BUT DOES IT ALL TASTE AS GOOD AS IT LOOKS?
OH, AND IT DOES!

GAG!

NICOLE, YOU'VE BEEN THE FRONTRUNNER SO FAR, BUT I'M SORRY TO SAY THIS COOKIE . . . HAS WAY TOO MUCH SALT!
I . . . I DIDN'T KNOW . . .
MADISON!
I DON'T KNOW WHAT YOU'RE UPSET ABOUT NICOLE. THE HEAD CHEF SHOULD TASTE EVERYTHING!
EVEN IF YOU'VE DONE IT A MILLION TIMES!
I'VE BEEN SABOTAGED! I DEMAND A REMATCH.

OKAY, EVERYONE, LET'S FIGURE THIS OUT!

MISTY SABOTAGED US WITH THE BRUSSELS SPROUTS.
SHE DUMPED SOME INTO OUR MIXER WHILE WE WEREN'T LOOKING.
WE WERE JUST GETTING A LITTLE JUSTICE.

SHE MIGHT HAVE DONE THAT TO US TOO.
NICOLE!
IS THIS TRUE? I WANT PROOF!
OF COURSE. THIS *IS* TELEVISION AFTER ALL!

I SWEAR THAT WAS THE ONLY THING I DID! IT WAS ALL JUST A JOKE! I KNEW I WOULD WIN ANYWAY.
WHAT ABOUT OUR CAKE? AND KURT AND CORRIE'S FLOWERS? THERE WERE NO CAMERAS IF IT WAS DONE OVERNIGHT.

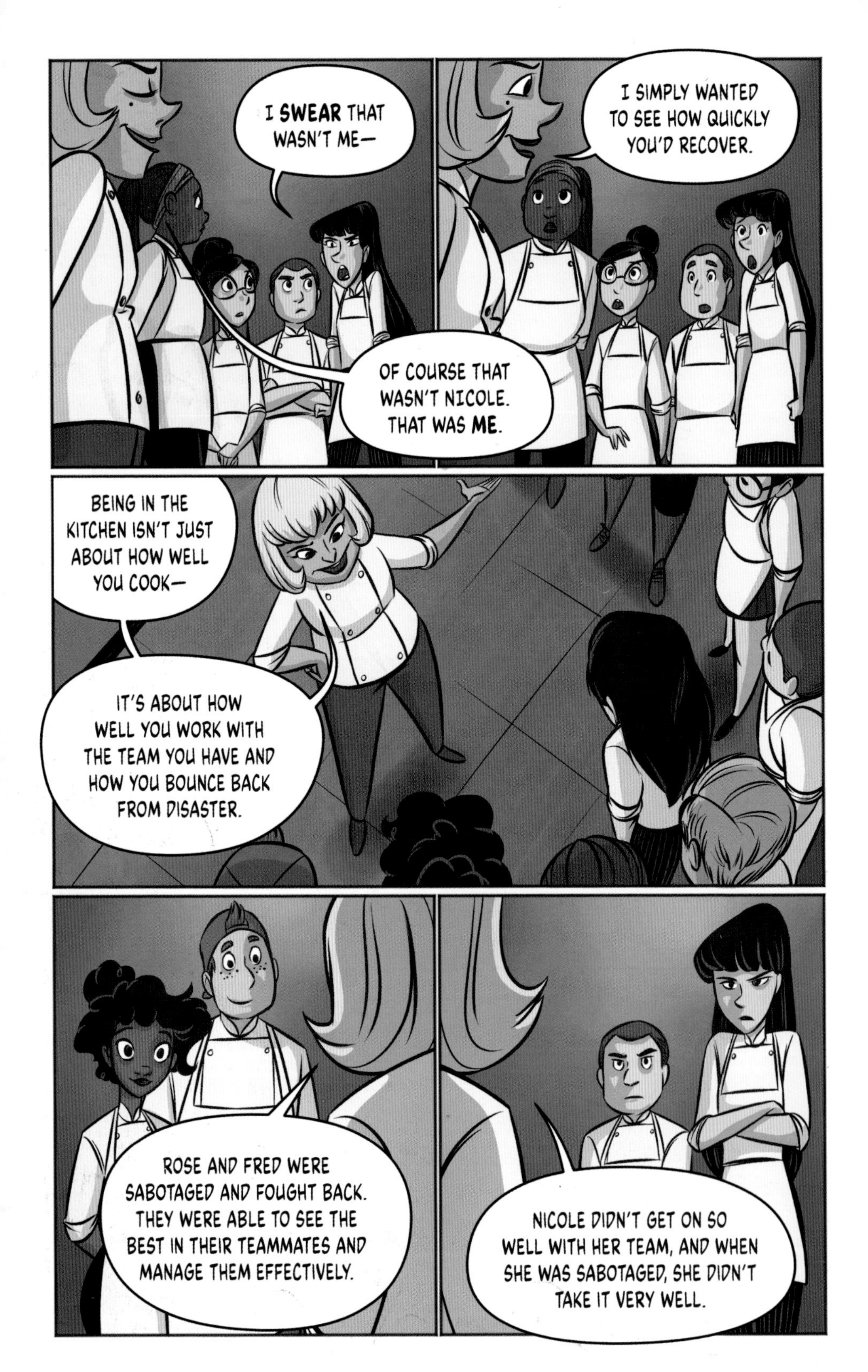
I SWEAR THAT WASN'T ME—
OF COURSE THAT WASN'T NICOLE. THAT WAS ME.
I SIMPLY WANTED TO SEE HOW QUICKLY YOU'D RECOVER.
BEING IN THE KITCHEN ISN'T JUST ABOUT HOW WELL YOU COOK—
IT'S ABOUT HOW WELL YOU WORK WITH THE TEAM YOU HAVE AND HOW YOU BOUNCE BACK FROM DISASTER.
ROSE AND FRED WERE SABOTAGED AND FOUGHT BACK. THEY WERE ABLE TO SEE THE BEST IN THEIR TEAMMATES AND MANAGE THEM EFFECTIVELY.
NICOLE DIDN'T GET ON SO WELL WITH HER TEAM, AND WHEN SHE WAS SABOTAGED, SHE DIDN'T TAKE IT VERY WELL.

FORGET IT! THIS ISN'T A CONTEST . . . THE WHOLE THING HAS BEEN A JOKE FROM THE START!
NICOLE!

THAT IS NOT HOW I TAUGHT YOU. WE ARE PROFESSIONALS, NOT CHEATERS!

ALL MY LIFE I'VE BEEN TRYING TO LIVE UP TO YOUR PERFECT IMAGE! WORKING SO HARD, ONLY TO HAVE IT THROWN AWAY, OR SPIT OUT LIKE GARBAGE. I'M SICK OF IT!

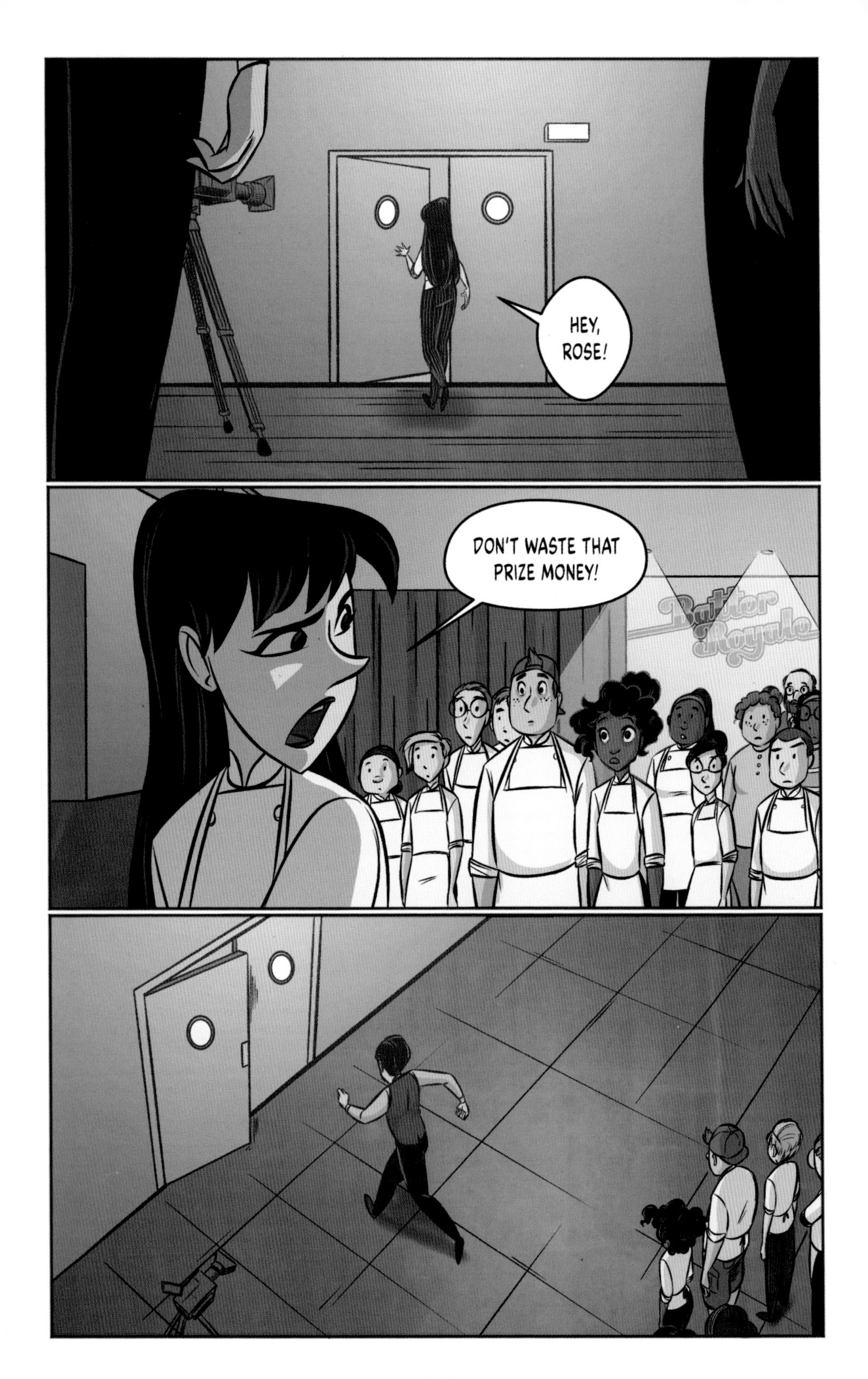
HEY, ROSE!
DON'T WASTE THAT PRIZE MONEY!
Batter Royale

LET HER GO.
NO, I WANT TO TALK TO HER.

1

UGH, WHAT DO YOU WANT?

I JUST WANTED TO ASK IF YOU'RE OKAY . . .
LOOK, I DON'T NEED YOU TO FEEL SORRY FOR ME. YOU WON!

I GET THAT YOU WANTED TO LIVE UP TO YOUR FAMILY NAME.
YEAH, AND I JUST RUINED OUR REPUTATION ON INTERNATIONAL TV!
I THINK YOU'LL RECOVER JUST FINE.
YOU SAYING YOU'RE UP FOR A REMATCH?
MAYBE . . . SOMEDAY! AS LONG AS THERE'S NO TRAP DOORS, OR KIDNAPPING.
I KNOW RIGHT? JUST COOKING.
DEAL.

Batter Royale
I'M HAPPY TO ANNOUNCE THAT ROSE AND FRED ARE THIS YEAR'S *BATTER ROYALE* CHAMPIONS! YOU WILL RECEIVE HALF A MILLION DOLLARS AND A BRILLIANT BOOK DEAL!

CONGRATS, HON! I KNEW YOU COULD DO IT.
THANKS DAD!

OF COURSE, WE ARE BOTH **SO** PROUD OF YOU.

OBVIOUSLY, IT'S A TALENT THAT COMES FROM MY SIDE.

UMM, I'M NOT SO SURE ABOUT THAT, JEFF.
NO REALLY! REMEMBER THAT ONE TIME I MADE RICE PUDDING? IT WAS PRETTY GOOD!

WHAT?

COUGH

YOU TWO WERE AMAZING!
WE HEARD THAT YOU WERE ACCEPTED INTO OUR SCHOOL IN CANADA, AND SO WE'VE DECIDED TO REWARD YOU WITH FULL TUITION FOR OUR DIPLOMA PROGRAM.

CONGRATULATIONS!

Directions

1. Bring ¼ cup of water, the sugar, and salt to a boil in a small saucepan while stirring.
2. Simmer on medium to low heat, stirring occasionally until the mixture eventually turns an amber color.
3. Add the cream and reduce heat to low.
4. Keep stirring occasionally to get rid of the foam.
5. Cook to a temperature of 200°F, or until the sauce becomes thick enough to coat a spoon.

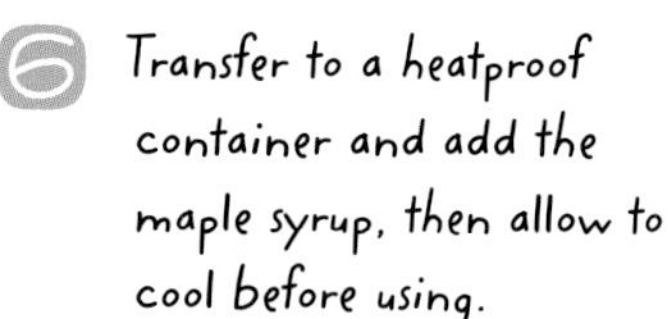

6. Transfer to a heatproof container and add the maple syrup, then allow to cool before using.

QUAYGA
GRAND RE-OPENING!
HI, CHEF! I MEAN, BONNIE!
HEY, ROSE! IF YOU'RE LOOKING FOR FRED, HE'S IN MY OFFICE.
THANKS!
HEY! HAVE YOU DECIDED WHERE TO GO YET?

NOT SURE. I WAS THINKING MAYBE SOMEWHERE IN EUROPE, BUT I HEAR THE FOOD SCENE IN JAPAN IS THE BEST!
SO . . . YOU'RE JUST GOING TO EAT YOUR WAY ACROSS THE GLOBE?
TRAVEL
YOU COULD COME WITH ME!
TEMPTING, BUT IF I DON'T GET MY COOKING DEGREE, MY PARENTS WILL KILL ME.
THEY WON'T REALLY.
YEAH, THEY LITERALLY WILL.
WELL, THAT SETTLES IT THEN!
WHAT?
I KNOW WHERE MY FIRST STOP WILL BE.
FIELDBERRY, HERE I COME!
EXCELLENT CHOICE.

The End

THANK YOUS:

To my fairy godmother agent, Adria Goetz
and Martin Literary Management for believing in me.

To Charlotte Greenbaum, Andrea Miller, and everyone at Abrams,
for taking my story on and helping to crank this book out,
you've made my dream come true!

To Andrew and Cat for helping produce this beast.

To John, for always being there for me and
supporting all of my weird creative whims.

To my kids, J.T. and Jason, for being my inspiration.

To the family, friends, and colleagues who supported my journey.

To Svetlana, Bianca, and Faith for the professional advice.

To everyone online, who has supported my work
and cheered me on over the years.

To Halifax and London, my two favorite cities,
and to Peggy Porschen Academy, for teaching me
how to bake and decorate cakes.

Finally, thank you to the Ontario Arts Council
for the grant support.